THIS IS
ESPIE SANCHEZ

by *Terry Dunnahoo*

E. P. Dutton & Co., Inc.
New York

Library of Congress Cataloging in Publication Data

Dunnahoo, Terry   This is Espie Sanchez

SUMMARY: A fifteen-year-old Explorer Scout's
sense of danger is aroused by the boyfriend of
a teenager she meets while helping at the
police station screening calls.

[1. Police—Fiction   2. Mexican Americans—Fiction]
I. Title.
PZ7.D92172Th   [Fic]   76-14807   ISBN 0-525-41130-5

Published simultaneously in Canada by Clarke,
Irwin & Company Limited, Toronto and Vancouver

Editor: Ann Durell
Designer: Meri Shardin
Printed in the U.S.A.   First Edition
10 9 8 7 6 5 4 3 2 1

To my sister Laurette, with love

Chapter 1

Espie answered the phone on the first ring. "Northeast Division, Explorer Sanchez speaking. May I help you, please?"

A woman said, "I don't want an Explorer. I want a policeman."

Espie glanced at Sergeant Ernie Jackson who was checking reports with the eraser part of his pencil pointed at every word. She said, "Ma'am, if you tell me what you want, maybe I can help you."

"I have a lion in my living room. Can you get rid of it?" the woman asked angrily.

"You have a lion in your living room?"

Sergeant Jackson frowned. "Mrs. Caldwell," he said to Espie, and picked up the receiver on his phone. "Good evening, Mrs. Caldwell. This is Sergeant Jackson."

"Why do you waste my time by letting those children answer the phone?" the woman asked. Espie stiffened. She'd be sixteen in May.

Sergeant Jackson said, "The Explorer Scouts take a lot of work off our backs. I think you should give them a chance."

The woman's voice rose. "Well, I have a lion locked up in my living room and that child can't get it out, can she?"

"Mrs. Caldwell, we don't have lions in Los Angeles."

"Maybe one escaped from the zoo."

"There's no lion missing from the zoo," Sergeant Jackson said. Espie wondered how he could be so patient.

"Are you sure?"

"We'd be the first to know."

"Then where did the lion in my living room come from?"

Sergeant Jackson smiled. "Mrs. Caldwell, is your television on?"

"Of course it's not on. I turned it off when I went to bed. The lion woke me up."

"Maybe you only *think* you turned off your television."

"You telling me I'm crazy?"

Sergeant Jackson sighed. "Mrs. Caldwell, the door to the living room is closed. Right?"

"You think I'd leave it open with a lion snarling at me?"

"I want you to go to the door and listen. Then come tell me what you hear. Okay?"

The woman hesitated, then said, "All right, but don't hang up on me."

Espie heard Mrs. Caldwell put down her receiver. The sergeant said to Espie, "She calls a couple of times a month. Lonely, I guess. Sometimes we send somebody out to talk to her and check her story. She comes up with wild ones."

Mrs. Caldwell picked up her telephone. "Why, it's just an old movie, Sergeant. How do you suppose I forgot to turn off the television?"

"We all forget things, Mrs. Caldwell. Good night." Sergeant Jackson put down his phone and Espie slammed hers into place. Her first night working the desk and she got a fruitcake.

The policeman said, "Hey, you're not going to let an old lady get to you, are you?"

Espie straightened the navy-blue skirt of her uniform. "I trained eight Saturdays at the police academy and I couldn't even handle my first call," she said.

Sergeant Jackson chuckled. "I went three months, five days a week and, after fifteen years on the force, I'm still not always sure how to answer a call." The sergeant picked up his pencil. "You'll handle it okay next time," he said.

Espie stared at the telephone and dared it to give her another chance. When it rang, she picked it up immediately. "Northeast Division, Explorer Sanchez speaking. May I help you, please?" she said in her best Academy manner.

A man said, "Yeah, you can help me. Make that damn police helicopter stop circling my house. I can't hear my television."

Espie heard the roar of the helicopter. "If a chopper is circling your area, the men are answering a call for help from one of our ground units."

"They're disturbing my peace."

Espie glanced at Sergeant Jackson. He was watching her. "Sir, the officers are doing their job." The noise from the other end of the line grew quieter. "They seem to be moving away," she said.

"Yeah, they are. Okay, I'll let them get away with it this time. But next time they come around here I'm going to have them arrested for disturbing the peace."

"It's your right, sir," Espie said, and put down the telephone.

Ernie Jackson said, "Sounds like you handled that one okay."

"A citizen complaining about our chopper."

Sergeant Jackson smiled. "You talk like a veteran policeman," he said.

Officers Gary Horton and Ron Peters came up the hall from the parking lot. A black-haired girl dressed in jeans and blouse walked between them. Espie noticed the hair first because it looked as if it had been hacked off. But the girl was beautiful and even the chopped-off hair didn't change that.

Sergeant Jackson asked, "What have you got?"

Officer Horton said, "A four eighty-four. The manager at Save-A-Lot Drugs caught her outside the store wearing a wig she didn't pay for."

Sergeant Jackson asked, "What happened to her hair?"

Ron Peters said, "She won't tell us."

The girl's hand went to her hair. One strand hung almost to her waist, as long as Espie's, but the rest was in short, ragged lengths.

Officer Horton touched the girl's arm. "Come on, Teresa. You'll have to wait in the holding tank while I call your parents."

Teresa said, "Don't call them. I'll never take anything again." Tears filled her eyes and spilled down her cheeks. She touched the long strand of hair. "My father will kill me."

Officer Horton touched her arm and eased her toward the holding tank. Espie watched the policeman open the door to the small room. Teresa walked in, still begging him not to call her parents. He closed the door and Espie shuddered. Seven months ago that same door had closed behind her after she had been picked up for running away from home.

Ron Peters said, "I'll call downtown to see if she has a record."

Officer Horton opened his note pad and dialed Teresa's number. "I wonder what happened to her hair," he said.

Espie looked toward the holding tank. She couldn't see Teresa's hair through the small glass window, but she saw her face. It wore a mask of fear.

Chapter 2

Officer Peters hung up. "There's no record on Teresa Hernandez. At least not one that fits our juvenile."

Gary Horton said into the phone, "Yes, you can see her, Mr. Hernandez. That's right, the police station on York Boulevard." He put down the phone. "He's coming right down."

Espie asked, "Did he sound mad?"

"He didn't sound happy."

"You know what I mean. Teresa said he'd kill her."

Peters asked, "When did you graduate from the Academy?"

Espie's hand went to the navy-blue ribbon tie at the neck of her long-sleeved white blouse. She knew the newness of her uniform made her look like a recent graduate. "Saturday. Why?" she said.

"After you've been around a while you'll learn almost all juveniles say that. We haven't had one come up dead yet." He stood up. "I'm going to get some coffee. Anybody want some?"

Sergeant Jackson shook his head. Gary Horton said,

"Yeah, bring me a cup." He took out his pencil. "I'll get started on this report."

Espie glanced toward the holding tank. Teresa still stared at them through fear-filled eyes. "Can't you let her out?" Espie asked. Officer Horton shook his head.

The phone rang and Espie answered it. A man said, "This is Edwin Tiller at Save-A-Lot Drugs. A couple of men picked up a girl here a while ago."

"Yes," Espie said.

"Well, listen, I've been thinking it over. It's only a few weeks before Christmas and all. I hate to, you know, I hate to get the kid in trouble." Espie tightened her grip on the phone. The man went on. "Will you tell the officers I don't want to press charges?"

Espie smiled. "Hold on, I'll let you talk to Officer Horton."

Gary Horton picked up the phone beside him and pressed the lighted button. After he listened, he said, "If you don't press charges, we'll have to let her go." He nodded while he listened. "Okay, Mr. Tiller, it's up to you. Yes, thank you. Merry Christmas to you, too." He hung up the phone and went to the holding tank. He opened the door. "Your father will be here in a few minutes. You can wait on the bench."

Teresa looked from him to Espie. Espie said, "The man dropped the charge against you."

For a moment some of the fear left Teresa's eyes. She sat on the bench and put her hand to her hair. All her fear returned.

She was still playing with the short strands when a man burst into the station followed by a sobbing woman. Teresa ran to her. The man yelled, "They did this to your hair? I'll kill them."

He ran toward the counter-like desk. Espie jumped out of the way. Teresa said "No, Papa. They didn't do it." He almost got over to the desk before Sergeant Jackson pushed his hand against Mr. Hernandez's face while Gary Horton ran to the other side of the desk and twisted the man's arm behind his back.

The policeman said, "We didn't touch her, Mr. Hernandez. Now, unless you calm down, we'll book you for assault on a police officer."

Espie saw the man's body relax. Gary Horton let go slowly. He said, "She won't tell us what happened to her hair."

Mr. Hernandez turned to Teresa, who pushed against her mother for protection. The woman looked much younger than her husband. He asked, "How did your hair get like this? Who did it?" He pulled her away from her mother. "Who did it?" he shouted.

Teresa yelled back at him, "I can't tell you." She began to cry. Long, hard sobs shook her body.

Her father's face softened. He put his arms around her and she buried her face in his jacket. "*Mi niña*, don't cry. Don't cry like this."

"Why did you take the wig?" Mrs. Hernandez asked. "You never did anything like this."

"I wanted to hide my hair."

Gary Horton said, "Look, Mr. Hernandez, the man at Save-A-Lot Drugs isn't going to press charges, so Teresa's free to go. She's had a rough night. Why don't you take her home?"

Mr. Hernandez wiped his cheek with the back of his hand, and Espie realized he had been crying, too. "I'm sorry about what I did," he said. He kept his arm around Teresa's shoulder. "Let's go home," he said.

Ron Peters came up the hall with the coffee. "What

happened?" he asked. Espie told him and he grinned. "See, I told you her father wouldn't kill her."

Espie glared at him and went to the desk where Officer Horton had been sitting. The policeman said, "Hey, don't take that report. I'm not finished with it."

"I was only going to find out where Teresa lives. I might go see her."

Officer Peters said, "Don't do it."

"Why not?"

"Because it isn't a good idea," the policeman told her.

Gary Horton said, "Ron is right, Espie. If you get too involved with people you meet in this business, you won't be able to do your job." He sat down and picked up his pencil. "Take Teresa, for instance. When I saw that kid at Save-A-Lot, she looked so scared and pitiful with her hair butchered up like that, I wanted to tell her everything would be all right. But I couldn't. She had broken the law and it was my job to arrest her."

"For a cheap wig," Espie said.

"Yes, for a cheap wig," Officer Horton said.

Ron Peters said, "If you're going to be a cop, you'll have to start thinking that way."

"Who said I was going to be a cop?"

Sergeant Jackson leaned back in his chair. "A lot of girls who become Explorers want to be officers."

"That's not why I joined," Espie said.

Officer Horton had finished his report. He gave it to Sergeant Jackson. "Come on, Ron, let's get back on the street." He stopped at the door. "Espie, forget Teresa. She'll be okay. Her father's hot-headed but he loves her. So does her mother." Espie nodded and he smiled. "Say, why *did* you become an Explorer?"

"So I could get out nights."

The policemen laughed and waved on their way down

the hall. Espie didn't try to tell them that really *was* the reason she had joined the group.

Sergeant Jackson said, "It's almost eleven. How are you getting home?"

"Carlos Medina will give me a ride after he closes the Christmas tree lot."

"I understand the Explorers made over three hundred dollars' profit selling trees last year."

"Sure did—paid for our trip to Disneyland Sunday." Espie smiled at the memory as she picked up Officer Horton's empty coffee cup and threw it in the trash basket. "I thought there would be more going on tonight."

"A lot of our calls are handled through the switchboard downtown. But Tuesdays are pretty quiet most places. If you want action, come on weekends."

Carlos strolled in. His khaki uniform looked as clean and starched as when he had picked her up at six thirty. His black hair hung just above his collar. "How did it go?" he asked Espie.

Sergeant Jackson answered for her. "She did great."

Espie smiled. Carlos was another reason she had become an Explorer.

The phone rang. Espie reached for it. Sergeant Jackson said, "I'll get it." Espie put on her uniform hat and her sweater. Some of the girls had navy-blue capes to match their uniforms, but Mrs. Garcia didn't have money to buy material to make one. Espie walked toward the door, but Carlos stopped her and pointed to Sergeant Jackson.

"How long since you've seen him, Mrs. Lerner?" the policeman asked. "I'll send a couple of cars right away," he said when he got his answer. He hung up. "A five-year-old boy has been missing since six o'clock and his mother calls at eleven." He shook his head and put the call out.

Carlos asked Espie, "Will Mrs. Garcia let you help look for him?"

Espie said, "I'll call and ask her." She dialed her number. Denise Manning, who shared her foster home, answered it with a sleepy hello. Espie asked, "Is Mrs. Garcia asleep?"

"Yes, she is. Why? What's the matter?" Denise asked. Espie liked Denise. A paddy had a rough time in the barrio, but Denise never complained.

"Carlos wants to help look for a missing boy. He wants to know if I can help."

"I guess it'll be okay. Sure. I'll leave a note for Mrs. Garcia in case she wakes up and checks on you." Espie hung up and told Carlos what Denise said. He had already written the information he needed in his notebook and had her running out the door before she could say good night to Sergeant Jackson.

Carlos's car was an old sedan he'd bought with the money he'd earned working at a taco stand. The car needed a paint job and the right front fender had been bashed in, but it started the moment he switched on the ignition. They turned up York Boulevard to Figueroa and drove south.

"Think we'll find him?" Espie asked.

Carlos stopped for a red light and tapped the steering wheel while he waited to move again. "The house is on Mt. Washington. It's hilly and there's a lot of brush. If he's slipped into one of the ravines, it'll be rough."

The light turned green and the car moved again. They eased onto Museum Drive and began to climb. The road curved and narrowed. The lights from the city lay below them. Carlos stopped behind two police cars. "Come on," he said as he got out of the car and ran up the stairs that led to the house.

Espie tried to get out on her side, but there was no sidewalk and she couldn't get the door open because of the high bushes. She was surprised at the country-like area only a few miles from where she lived. She eased out Carlos's side and ran to catch up to him. When she reached the house he was already talking to a sergeant bent over a map of the area. The bright light from the police helicopter overhead lit up the hill. The sergeant asked, "Have you had search-and-rescue training?"

Carlos said, "I have, but Explorer Sanchez hasn't. I'll keep her with me."

"Do you have a flashlight?" the man asked.

Carlos said, "I have a couple in the car."

"Okay, the kid is wearing a red shirt and brown corduroy pants. He was last seen around six o'clock playing on the porch with his dog. The dog's with him. That's lucky, because if the boy went to sleep someplace the dog will bark. The kid's name is Mark and the dog is just called Mutt. Mrs. Lerner checked all the neighbors. Most of them are out searching now. If you find anything, blow your whistle until we get to you." He rolled up the map. "Look under porches, in back yards." His voice changed when he said, "And swimming pools."

Carlos started down the stairs. "Do you have a whistle?" he asked. Espie shook her head. "I have an extra one. You better take it in case we get separated."

Espie said, "You sound like the drill sergeants at the Academy."

Carlos smiled. "Sorry." He gave her a flashlight and she put the whistle chain around her neck. "Come on. Our area is over here," Carlos said. He called Mark's name and directed his own flashlight into the bushes. Espie crossed the street and did the same on her side.

When the helicopter flew directly above them, its light

lit up the ground like daylight, but when it moved away darkness surrounded them. Espie tripped. The straight skirt and black-heeled shoes she wore weren't made for walking on uneven ground. When Denise had gone on her search-and-rescue training she had worn jeans and tennis shoes.

Espie turned into the first yard. She kept her light on the ground and called Mark's name. She shivered. It had been a warm day in Los Angeles, but now it was damp and cold. Her light hit concrete, then water. She knew she had to look in the pool. She moved the light slowly. The water shimmered beneath it. "Please, God, don't let him be in there," she said.

When she reached the other end she realized she had been holding her breath. She let it out. The chopper came toward her and lighted up the yard. She checked the pool again, then walked over the gravel path to the front of the house and saw Carlos's light already searching under the side of his second house. She hurried so she wouldn't get too far behind him.

The next house was surrounded by a low wall. When she reached the back, she flashed her light on the other side. There was a ravine dotted with low trees and mesquite. If Mark had fallen down there, she wouldn't be able to see him. She called his name, then called Mutt. She thought her voice echoed through the hills, but it was other voices calling Mark and his dog. With so many people looking, someone would find him soon.

She went around house after house. Few people came out to see what she was doing. Espie decided most of them were searching. Her feet hurt. She felt a blister on her heel. Her hands were so cold she could hardly hold the flashlight. Carlos didn't slow down and she half ran on her side of the street to keep up with him. They had walked so far from Mark's house, the helicopter didn't circle above them anymore. She didn't want to be left alone in the dark. She moved faster.

The next house looked abandoned. Ivy grew into the street. A shade banged against a broken window. She tripped and fell against the house. Her hand touched silk-sticky threads.

She turned her light on them. She had broken a spider's web. She shivered and wiped the threads on the ivy before she remembered ivy was full of snails. She rubbed her hand against her skirt and shook, both from the cold and from the web's threads that clung to her hand.

She called Mark's name while she ran to the back of the house. Her light fell on a bedspring, a chair with its insides pulled out, and moved to a table with only two legs. She ran her light to the back door. The screen was torn. She went up the wooden steps and looked inside. A refrigerator stood in the otherwise empty room. The screen door opened at her touch. The refrigerator drew her to it. She opened it. A dog fell on her feet.

Chapter 3

Espie pulled Mark from the refrigerator. He wasn't breathing. She put down her flashlight and stretched him on the floor. She pushed his chin up until his head fell back, then put her fingers over his nostrils and put her mouth on his, the way the Red Cross instructor had taught her at the Academy. She breathed into Mark's mouth and looked to see if his chest rose. It didn't. If she were doing it right, his chest would move.

Espie tried to remember her lesson on mouth-to-mouth resuscitation. How many times was she supposed to blow air into the victim? Twelve times a minute? That was for grown-ups. Twenty times. That was it. The instructor had used a rubber dummy to demonstrate. "Blow air in your victim, listen for air return, and look for chest movement." Espie did it over and over again before Mark's chest moved. She remembered Carlos and blew her whistle before she pushed more air into Mark's lungs.

Minutes later she heard Carlos in the yard. "Espie, where are you? Espie?"

"In the house," Espie shouted.

Carlos opened the door and turned his light on her. "I'll

get an ambulance," he said, and ran out. She heard his whistle again and again while she worked over Mark.

A siren filled the hills and died to a moan in front of the house. An ambulance, she thought. The instructor had said, "Continue first aid until a doctor or a trained person arrives."

The sergeant opened the door. "Here, let me do that," he said.

"Where's the doctor?" Espie asked.

"We've called an ambulance," the officer said, and tried to pull her away.

Espie stayed down. Two more policemen came in and people crowded in behind them. The officers tried to clear the room and the sergeant knelt beside Espie. "Let me try," he said. She moved away and he took over. She felt dizzy when she stood up and, for a moment, thought she was going to faint. She leaned against the wall and watched the man blow air into Mark, who still lay unmoving except for the rising and falling of his chest.

Espie heard a siren far below them. It became louder, faded, and got louder again as the ambulance followed the long, steep curves. It stopped in front of the house and she heard running feet. A man in white went down beside Mark. He felt for a pulse and listened for a heartbeat. "He's dead," he said.

The sergeant nodded. "I figured he was, but I was hoping for a miracle."

Espie moved toward Mark. "He's not dead." Carlos held her back while the men put the boy on the stretcher. She broke away from Carlos and picked up Mutt. His fur was soft, but his body was stiff and cold. She carried him to the stretcher and put him beside Mark.

The sergeant said, "Let's get outside. I'll take your statement, then give you a ride back to your car." The other officers cleared a path for them through the crowd that seemed reluctant to leave.

When they reached the squad car, the sergeant questioned Espie and she answered with as few words as possible. She had to get away before the tears came. It wasn't until she was in Carlos's car on the way down the hill that she realized she hadn't seen Mrs. Lerner. Neighbors must have kept her away from the abandoned house. Espie didn't even know if there was a Mr. Lerner. Gary Horton had told her not to get involved. How could she help it?

Carlos said, "If I'd known it was going to end this way I wouldn't have taken you with me." The tires screeched as he took a curve too fast. "I've helped police search for six people in the past two years and, except for the one who had broken his leg, they were all okay when we found them."

Espie stared through the windshield at the deserted street. Her throat hurt from holding back tears. She began to shake. A moment later she had no control over her body. Carlos said, "Hey, you okay?"

"I'm freezing," Espie said.

Carlos pressed harder on the gas pedal. He was speeding, something he'd never done with her in the car. "I'll have you home in a couple of minutes."

When he stopped in front of Mrs. Garcia's house, Espie opened the door and held onto it until she knew her legs wouldn't buckle under her. Carlos eased out of the car behind her. "I'll be all right," she said, and pushed him gently down to the seat.

"You sure?"

Espie said, "The lights are on. Mrs. Garcia is up." Carlos got back in the car and Espie hurried up the walk to the house.

The door opened before she reached it. Mrs. Garcia

said, "Espie, you are all right?" Espie closed the door and leaned against it. Tears spilled out even before she heard Carlos drive away. She was still shaking. Mrs. Garcia said, "I have soup. You eat and get warm."

Espie shook her head. Vomit filled her mouth and she ran to the bathroom. Again she had no control over the body that made attempts to vomit even after there was nothing left to get up.

Mrs. Garcia said, "I get Denise. We go to the hospital."

Espie straightened up. "No, I'm okay." Her reflection looked back at her from the mirror of the medicine cabinet. Her tangled hair framed a dirty tear-streaked face. She stumbled to the living room and dropped to the couch.

Mrs. Garcia sat beside her, and Espie told her about Mark. She told her how scared she'd been when she thought he might be in the pool, how she'd been afraid to be left behind in the dark. Once she started to talk, she couldn't stop. She told her how Mark's mouth had felt, how she had tasted chocolate on his lips, how she had been so certain she'd make him breathe again. "And I couldn't do it," she said.

Mrs. Garcia put her arm around her. "That is God's job."

Espie pulled away from her. "Why the hell didn't He do it, then?"

"Esperanza!"

Espie got up from the couch and almost fell down before she moved toward the room she shared with Denise. "I have to go to bed or I won't be able to get up for school."

"It is almost four o'clock. You will be too tired for school," Mrs. Garcia said. Her face still reflected the shock of Espie's question about God.

"I have to go. One of the Explorer rules is that we don't let police business get in the way of school work."

"But you are too tired for school."

"I'll be okay after a couple of hours' sleep," Espie said. She opened the bedroom door and heard Denise's even breathing. Espie put on the small light over her bed and undid the brass buttons on her uniform vest. She took off her blouse and skirt and sat on the bed. Her shoes were scratched and covered with dirt. Large holes dotted her pantyhose. She pulled them off and lay across the bed in her slip, too exhausted to even put on her pajamas.

When she woke up, the sun was bright behind the drawn shade and she had a blanket over her. Denise was gone. Espie looked at the clock on the bureau and ran to the kitchen. Mrs. Garcia was stirring something in a large pan. Espie said, "It's almost noon. Why didn't you wake me up?"

"You were too tired," Mrs. Garcia said. Her hair was combed and knotted at the neck. Her black dress covered her body like a tent.

"I can still make sixth period. I have a math test," Espie said, and ran to her room for her jeans and T-shirt. She brushed her hair and hurried to the bathroom to wash her face. What could she write on the note to explain her absence? Mrs. Garcia wouldn't lie. Espie brushed her teeth and went back to her room for her books. "I'll need a note," she said when she got back to the kitchen.

Mrs. Garcia said, "You must eat before school." Espie reached for the bread and put two slices in the toaster. "You must eat more. I fix eggs."

"No, I'll eat the toast on the way to school." She took out a sheet of note paper and searched for the best words for her excuse. Finally she wrote, "Espie did not go to school this morning because she threw up during the night." She put it in front of Mrs. Garcia for her signature. Mrs. Garcia read it and signed it. She wouldn't lie, but she wouldn't take a chance on Espie being suspended from the Explorers, either.

Espie put the two pieces of toast together and ate them like a sandwich on the way up Daly Street. She wasn't all that crazy about school, but she had to keep a C average to stay in the Explorer program. There had been rap sessions at the meetings about a trip to the mountains and a weekend in San Diego. Espie wanted to go. And there was Carlos. She didn't want to take the chance of being kicked out.

A small boy on a tricycle reminded her of Mark. He could be doing that today if she had found him sooner. No, it wasn't her fault. His mother should have called earlier. It didn't matter whose fault it was. Mark was dead. And if that refrigerator hadn't been there, maybe he'd be alive. She saw a clock in the window of a gas station and walked faster.

Last night seemed so long ago, she had almost forgotten Teresa. Espie wondered what had happened to the girl's hair and what her father had done to her when he got her home. Don't get involved, she told herself as she ran up the school steps lined with kids who had second lunch period.

Someone said, "Look at the piglet run. Hey, piggy-wiggly, did you learn that at the pig-sty?"

Espie ignored them the way she had the day before. At the Academy she'd been yelled at and insulted to see if she could hold her temper if people called her names while she worked crowd control at parades and fiestas. "An Explorer will not act in any way that will bring shame to her uniform or the uniform of the Los Angeles Police Department." That's what she'd learned in the classroom at the

Academy. And Denise had warned her to expect name-calling in school, but Espie didn't believe kids would bother her because she was Mexican like almost everybody else at Franklin Heights. She had told Denise, "They call you names because you're a paddy."

Denise had said, "A pig is a pig. Nationality doesn't matter."

If the kids wanted her to fight they'd be disappointed. She didn't fight. It wasn't because she was the patron saint of the barrio, but because, at five foot two inches tall and ninety-two pounds, almost everybody was bigger than she was, and she was too smart to get herself batted around.

She hurried past two guys having a fist fight. A couple didn't even look up from a heavy love session to see what was going on. A boy at the end of the hall nodded from too many reds. And a girl took a swig of vodka. Security guards patrolled the school, but the students' warning system let the kids know when guards were heading their way.

The sixth-period bell rang before she reached the attendance office. She hurried in, gave the note to the student on duty, and ran up the stairs to her second-floor classroom.

When she entered, a paper airplane flew over her head and landed on the teacher's desk. He called for order. Espie sat down behind a girl who asked her where she'd been. "I was sick during the night," Espie said.

The second bell quieted the kids enough to allow the teacher to be heard. "You're using up your exam time," he said. A few kids ignored him, but most of them stopped talking, and he passed out the test papers. Groans came from different parts of the room. Espie looked at her paper and joined in the groaning session. Twenty problems. Stupid questions. Always stupid questions about things she'd never have to know. The teacher ignored the complaints and picked up a copy of *Playboy*. When the bell rang, Espie turned in her paper, certain she had lost her C average.

She worried about it during English while the teacher explained the meaning of the words in their spelling books. A boy asked, "Hey, do I have to know these words to be a gas jockey?"

"No, but you might need them to fill out the job application," the teacher said.

"What job application? You tell the dude you can find a gas tank and he hires you."

The teacher continued to explain the words as though they were the most important things in the world. Espie ignored her until she heard a word she hadn't recognized in her math test. She paid attention after that, but the minute the bell rang, she ran out with the rest of the kids. She looked for Denise and spotted her across the campus. She was easy to see. Her blond hair stood out in the crowd of mostly Mexicans and two or three dozen Orientals.

When Espie caught up with her, Denise asked, "When did you get here?"

"Sixth period. Why didn't you wake me up?"

"Mrs. Garcia wouldn't let me. She told me about last night. That was rough." Denise shifted her books from one arm to the other. "I think I would have panicked and forgotten everything I learned in first aid."

Espie couldn't imagine Denise in a panic. She didn't let things bother her. Or, if she did, she didn't let it show. Espie was telling her about Teresa when a couple of dudes shoved them against a wall. One of them said, "Look at that. A white piglet and a brown piglet."

Denise said, "Oink, oink." The guys laughed, and the

one with a torn knitted cap pulled down over his ears said, "Man, she even sounds like a pig."

Espie swore at them in Spanish. Denise pulled her away. "Don't let them know it bothers you. They'll quit."

Espie said, "I may have to learn to fight."

"Not while I'm around. I'm too much of a coward."

The WALK sign came on across the street and they stepped off the curb. A pickup truck swerved around the corner and almost hit them. Espie jumped back. "Hey, Teresa was in there with some guy."

"You sure?"

"Her hair was cut short, all even and everything, but it was her." They started across the street. "You know, she looked even more scared than she did last night."

Chapter 4

Espie told Denise how Officer Horton acted when Espie tried to get Teresa's address from his report. "He told me not to get involved."

"He's right. You're going to meet hundreds of people while you're on duty. If you get involved in all their lives, you won't be able to live yours."

A wino in front of them picked up a half-smoked butt from the gutter and put it in his mouth. His laceless shoes slapped against his naked heels as he walked to a man waiting for a bus and asked for a light.

Espie said, "Well, nobody's going to stop me from getting involved in Mark's life." She pushed a strand of hair behind her shoulder. "I mean his . . . death," she half whispered.

Denise asked, "What can you do?"

"I don't know," Espie said. They turned off Daly onto a street lined with bungalows no better or worse than the other houses in the barrio. "Maybe there should be a law against death traps like that refrigerator."

"There is. People are supposed to take the doors off refrigerators and freezers before they leave them outside."

"How about in empty houses?"

"I don't know about that."

Espie said, "The Explorers should do something."

"Like what?"

"Like letting people know about that law. I bet nobody on this street knows about it."

Denise said, "You're probably right."

"Then let's go from door to door and tell them."

"You mean you and me or the Explorers?"

"The Explorers. They're always looking for ways to help people."

They turned up the walk to Mrs. Garcia's house. Denise said, "Why don't you bring it up at the meeting Thursday night?"

Espie opened the door. "I will," she said.

Carlos called her that night to see how she felt, and he picked her and Denise up Thursday to take them to the meeting. Espie got in the back seat and Denise sat in front. They would switch on the way home. Nobody had said anything about who sat where, but somehow things had happened that way, and Espie was glad for the chance to be near Carlos. He seemed to like her all right, but, except for the meetings and the Explorer activities, she seldom saw him. His whole life was the Explorers and his job at the taco stand that helped his mother pay the rent and kept gas in his car.

When they reached the police station Carlos went in the roll-call room and Espie and Denise headed for the captain's office, where the girls held their meetings. When they passed the community-relations office, Officer Mary Parks called them in. Espie thought Parks looked great in her uniform, but she usually wore civilian clothes, like the green dress she had on now. "I got a memo on you, Espie," she said.

"What about?"

"Last night. The sergeant wrote you acted calm and professional under a crisis situation. I'm going to put it in your folder. It'll help you when you become eligible for your sergeant's stripes."

Espie didn't want any part of being a sergeant, a lieutenant, or a captain. She didn't like the way they yelled orders all the time. But she was pleased about the memo.

Denise said, "Espie has an idea for an Explorer project."

Mary Parks glanced at her watch. "Great, we'll talk about it at the meeting." They went down the hall to the captain's office. About two dozen girls waited around a small conference table.

Mary Parks led them in the pledge to the flag, then sat behind the captain's desk. "Roxanne, will you take roll call, please?" she said.

The girl called out a name. Its owner stood up. "Here, ma'am," she said. Roxanne called another name. "Here, ma'am," the girl said. Roxanne called Espie's name. Espie stood up and said, "Here, ma'am." She slouched back in her chair and watched the others jump up and down like yo-yos. She hated saying ma'am. She hated it here and she hated it at the Academy when she had to say ma'am and sir to Explorers just a year or two older than she was.

Captain Alice Eliott, with not a red hair out of place, watched the roll call from her place beside Mary Parks. The police officer was the group's sponsor and was present only to observe. Alice ran the meeting and she ran it tough. Espie thought about the memo. Maybe she'd try for sergeant's stripes. She could work her way up to captain. Then she wouldn't have to say ma'am to anybody.

After Roxanne finished with the roll call, the treasurer collected dues. There was always an argument about who

26

had paid and who hadn't. Espie wondered where Mrs. Garcia got the money for Espie's and Denise's dues, but no matter how little home sewing she took in, Mrs. Garcia came up with the dollar they each needed for the month.

After the dues collection, they discussed their trip to the children's ward at the county hospital.

Alice said, "We'll go to the hospital from here next Thursday. And don't forget your presents for the kids." She looked at Denise. "Explorer Manning, did Mrs. Garcia finish the Santa Claus suit?"

Denise jumped to her feet. "Yes, ma'am," she said.

"Very good. Bring it next week. And everybody in uniform." Alice smiled. "Except me, of course, because I'm going to be Santa Claus." Denise sat down and Alice asked, "Any new business?"

Denise turned to Espie, but Espie didn't get up. She hated to talk in front of a group of people. Denise nudged her, and Espie raised her hand only because she felt so strongly about Mark's death.

Alice said, "Explorer Sanchez."

Espie stood up and told them about Mark. She twisted a strand of hair around her finger. She shouldn't have started that way. She should have just told them about the law. Her throat was dry.

Alice interrupted her. "What are you leading up to, Sanchez?"

"There's a law against leaving doors on refrigerators and freezers when they're thrown out. People don't know that. I thought we could go from door to door and tell them."

Alice asked, "Does anybody think it's a worthwhile project?" Denise raised her hand. So did a lot of other girls. Alice walked to a wall lined with maps of the Northeast Division. "How many areas can we cover?"

One girl said, "I can do the area around Avenue 42."

Another said, "I can cover the streets around Garvanza."

Girls gave the location they would work and Alice stuck pins in the center of each. She didn't stop the girls from talking without being officially recognized, and Espie knew that meant even Alice thought the project was a good idea. Espie and Denise took an area in their neighborhood, and by the time the meeting closed at nine, every girl except two, who had to work over the weekend, had volunteered.

Espie felt pretty good about the outcome of her first Explorer suggestion. She slipped in beside Carlos and told him about it on the way home. There was no speeding the way there had been Tuesday night. He kept the speedometer at thirty-five and piloted the car easily through the light traffic.

She watched his face, shadowed by the dashboard lights. His black hair glistened every time they passed a street lamp. She leaned against the door and stared at him. He wasn't the best-looking guy she'd ever met, but he was the hardest to be with.

The next day her math teacher returned the test papers. He had written on hers, "This is barely a C. You'll have to work harder." Espie shoved the paper in her notebook. She had done the best she could.

The teacher leaned against his desk. "More than half of you failed that exam. I'm going to throw away all those F's and give you another chance. Those who are satisfied with their grades can stay with them. Those who think they can do better can try. But if you take the test, the second grade will be the one that counts on your report card. How many want to take the test?" Almost everybody raised their hands. Espie kept hers on the desk. She wasn't satisfied with her grade, but she was going to stick with it. Math was her worst subject.

Saturday morning she and Denise left the house at nine o'clock after Mrs. Garcia had fixed them egg chilaquiles and made the girls promise to walk around the blocks in a way that would bring them back to the house for lunch.

Denise crossed the street and went up the steps to her first house, and Espie covered her side. When they reached the corner they walked in opposite directions, and soon Denise had disappeared around a turn in the road.

It didn't take Espie long to cover houses on her street because most people knew she was an Explorer, but as she got farther from home, she had to answer as many questions about her uniform as she did about the law she wanted to talk about. It slowed her down, and she wished she'd worn jeans.

As she walked, she dodged kids on tricycles, kids on skates, kids in wagons, and the barking dogs that jumped around them. By the time the church bell chimed ten o'clock, the sun was hot on her back, she was thirsty, and her shoes were rubbing blisters next to the Band-Aids she wore over the blisters she got while she looked for Mark.

When she asked for a glass of water at the next house, the woman offered her breakfast. "I've had breakfast, thank you," Espie said.

The woman frowned. "Then you have lunch," she said while Espie drank the water.

Espie shook her head. The woman turned on a stove burner, held a tortilla over the flame, and put butter on it. "Then you take a tortilla."

Espie smiled. "Thank you," she said, and hurried to the next house. At eleven o'clock she started to work her way toward home. She turned the corner, walked past a nicely tailored lawn, and knocked on the door of a house that looked newly painted.

When the door opened, Espie stared at the girl who stood before her. The face was as beautiful as it had been Tuesday night, but the hair was wrong. At least it was wrong on this girl.

"Aren't you Teresa Hernandez?" Espie asked. Teresa started to close the door. "Wait. I want to talk to you."

Teresa held the door open a little. "You can't do anything to me. The man dropped the charge."

Espie said, "I know. I was there, remember?"

Teresa looked at Espie's uniform. "What are you? And what do you want?"

"I'm an Explorer and I'm not here about the other night." Espie stared at Teresa's hair. It fell below her shoulders.

Teresa put her hand up. "It's a wig. My boyfriend gave it to me."

"It looks nice," Espie said. She didn't know much about wigs, but she had seen cheap ones on some of the girls at school and they didn't look like Teresa's.

The girl said, "It's real hair."

A man's voice asked, "Who is it, Teresa?"

Teresa's hand jerked away from her hair and she turned toward the voice. "It's a girl. She wants . . ." She looked back at Espie. "What *do* you want?"

A man came to the door. He was well built, with a large chest and a narrow waist that made him look as though he were holding his breath. He looked at Espie's uniform. "What are you?" he asked, and Espie made up her mind to wear jeans after lunch.

"I'm an Explorer and I'm telling people about a law they may be breaking without knowing about it."

The man put his arm around Teresa. She moved away slightly and he pulled her back. "There's a lot of laws like that," he said. He turned from Espie and waved to somebody inside. "I'll see you when I get back from Tijuana," he said.

A woman's voice said good-bye, and the man kissed Teresa on the cheek. "I'll pick you up after school Monday," he said before he strolled down the walk to the pickup truck Espie had seen Teresa in Wednesday. Only now there was a camper shaped like a small house on the back.

"That your brother?" Espie asked.

Teresa rubbed her arm. The man had held it so tightly, his hand print still showed. "He's my boyfriend, Raul Torres," Teresa said.

Espie looked back at the truck moving out of its parking space. Espie had thought the man was thirty or thirty-five, but she must have been wrong because Teresa was only fifteen or sixteen.

Mrs. Hernandez came to the door. "Teresa, you're lucky to have such a good man." The woman didn't seem to recognize Espie, and she decided Mrs. Hernandez had been too upset Tuesday night to notice her. Teresa was still rubbing her arm.

Espie said, "I'd better tell you what I came for."

Mrs. Hernandez said, "Why don't you come in?"

Espie said, "No, I don't have time. I just . . ."

Teresa interrupted her. "Please come in," she said. Her voice said she needed a friend.

Espie said, "Okay, but I can't stay long." She entered the nicely decorated living room. The furniture all went together, nothing like Mrs. Garcia's house where none of the chairs matched. Plants stood everywhere. There were even some in bottles. A picture of Teresa dressed in the uniform of the local Catholic school hung between pictures of St. Martin de Porres and Our Lady of Guadalupe.

"You go to Holy Trinity?" Espie asked. Teresa nodded, "That's why I never saw you at Franklin Heights," Espie said.

Mrs. Hernandez pointed to a green and white striped chair. "Sit down, please." Espie was glad to get off her blistered feet. She sat in the chair and eased off her shoes while she told them about Mark's death and the law that should have prevented it.

When she finished, Teresa pointed to Espie's uniform. "I still don't know what you are," she said.

Espie sighed and explained for about the fortieth time that day that she was an Explorer and the group was part of the Boy Scouts organization.

Mrs. Hernandez asked, "How can you be part of the Boy Scouts if you're a girl?"

"It's a special group," Espie said. She smiled. "Besides, the girls are really called L.E.E.G.s, which stands for Law Enforcement Explorer Group."

Teresa asked, "How do you get to be a L.E.E.G.?"

Espie said, "I really have to go. See, I have to cover a lot more houses today." She forced her shoes back on. "Why don't you come with me? Then I can tell you about the Explorers and you can have lunch at my house."

Teresa jumped to her feet. "Great. I don't have anything to do now that Raul's gone."

"That Raul is a saint. He's always doing nice things. Now he's gone to Tijuana again to bring things to the poor. Teresa is lucky to have such a good man," Mrs. Hernandez said.

"Let's go," Teresa said.

Espie limped toward the door. "Wait a minute. I can't

walk with these shoes." She took them off, picked up her skirt and pulled off her pantyhose.

Mrs. Hernandez said, "I'll get a bag."

Espie put her shoes and pantyhose in it. "This is the only way to walk," she said.

Mrs. Hernandez laughed, but Teresa waited at the door without a smile. Espie said good-bye and followed Teresa out. "You have a nice house," she said.

"Raul paid a couple of guys to paint it."

When they reached the sidewalk, Espie asked, "What does he think of your hair? I mean, what did he say when he saw it cut?"

Teresa looked away. "He's the one who cut it off," she said.

Chapter 5

Espie stopped in the middle of the sidewalk. "Raul cut your hair short the way it is under the wig?" she asked Teresa.

Teresa stared at her. "How did you know my hair had been cut?"

"I saw you Wednesday with Raul. He almost ran over my friend and me."

Teresa said, "He was mad because I took the wig from Save-A-Lot."

Espie went up the walk to the house next to Teresa's. She had to answer the questions about the Explorers again. And this time she also had to explain why she was barefoot while she had on a uniform.

When she turned from the door, she told Teresa, "I'll come back after lunch in my jeans." She dodged a boy on a skateboard and asked Teresa, "Is Raul a barber?"

"My aunt cut my hair."

"Then why did you say Raul cut it?"

"He . . . Never mind."

Espie walked in silence. She gasped. "You mean he cut it Tuesday night?" Teresa nodded. "How?"

"With a . . . No, you'll tell the police," Teresa said.

"This uniform doesn't make me a fink."

Teresa looked at her as though she wanted to believe her. "He cut it with a knife," Teresa said finally.

"Why?"

"I told him I didn't want to go with him anymore. He grabbed my hair and sliced it off. He said if he couldn't have me nobody'd want me."

"Why didn't you tell the police?"

"I was too scared."

"Of the police?"

"Of Raul. He's slapped me around a couple of times."

"Did you tell your parents?"

"They wouldn't believe me. You heard my mother. 'Teresa is lucky to have such a good man.' " Teresa mimicked her mother's voice. "Hey, don't tell your mother about Tuesday night. She might not understand."

"I don't live with my mother. I live in a foster home." Espie smiled for the first time since she left Teresa's house. "And you don't have to worry about my foster mother not understanding. Her bureau is covered with pictures of girls she helped. And most of them came from the Northeast Police Station. I even came from there."

"You?"

Espie nodded. "Seven months ago I was in the same holding tank you were in Tuesday night."

"But you're an Explorer."

"I wasn't then. The cops picked me up for running away from home. My mother was always drunk and her boyfriends slapped me around, so I took off to look for my father. I was heading for Mexico, but I never made it." They turned a corner. "Denise Manning was working the desk that night and she said I should stay with her and Mrs. Garcia. The officer called her and she told the police to bring me over. I was going to run away from there, but . . ." Espie let her words trail off and looked at Teresa. "I've never told that to anybody. Only Denise and Mrs. Garcia know."

Teresa said, "I'm glad you told me. It makes me feel better. I don't mean I feel better because you've had trouble with the police. I m-mean . . ." she stammered.

Espie laughed. "I know what you mean."

When they entered Mrs. Garcia's house, Denise was already at the table eating a hamburger. Espie asked, "How did you beat me here?"

"I kept getting so many questions about my uniform, I skipped the rest of my area until I change clothes." She looked at Espie's feet. "What happened to your shoes?"

Espie held up the bag. "I'm going to have to break them in slowly." She introduced Teresa. When Denise heard the name, she stared at the girl's hair. Espie shot Denise a look and shook her head.

Mrs. Garcia asked, "You eat with us, Teresa?" Espie knew it would be this way. Mrs. Garcia always wanted people to eat, always wanted to make them fat.

Teresa said, "Yes, thank you."

Mrs. Garcia said, "I have hamburgers and I have chile. You want each one?"

Teresa said, "Just a hamburger, please."

Espie said, "I'll have both," and Mrs. Garcia smiled.

She put the meat in the frying pan. "You go to Franklin Heights?" she asked Teresa.

Teresa sat on one of the unmatched chairs. "No. I go to Holy Trinity."

Mrs. Garcia spooned chile in a bowl and put it in front of Espie. "I wish Espie and Denise go there, but I do not have the money. You have drugs in the school?"

"Not much," Teresa said.

When they finished eating, Espie went to her room to change. Denise followed her. "What's with Teresa's hair?" she asked as soon as they reached the room.

"It's a wig. Her boyfriend bought it for her." Espie took off her uniform and reached for her jeans.

"It looks like real hair. I bet it cost a lot."

Espie shrugged. "I guess so," she said. If Denise wanted more information, she wouldn't get it from her.

She went back to the kitchen, where Mrs. Garcia was talking about how much drugs there were in Franklin Heights.

"I am worried. I am always worried," she told Teresa.

"Ready to go?" Espie asked Teresa. The girl got up and thanked Mrs. Garcia for the hamburger.

When they got outside, Teresa said, "She's sure scared of drugs."

"Well, she doesn't have to worry about me. I tried them a couple of years ago. They're bummers."

Teresa asked a lot of questions about the Explorers during the afternoon. Finally, Espie told her, "We're going to County General next Thursday night instead of having our regular meeting. Why don't you come with us? We're going to sing carols and give the kids toys and candy."

Teresa thought about it while they walked up to a house with peeling paint and broken windows covered with foil. "Thursday?" she said. "Yeah, I can go. That's the night Raul goes out for beer and plays pool with his friends." She said it with such acceptance, Espie wondered how a guy could have so much control over a girl.

At four o'clock Teresa said she couldn't walk another step. Espie laughed. "You're too soft. What you need is eight Saturdays of physical torture at the police academy. It'll make you strong and tough like me."

Teresa smiled. "Could be, but I'm quitting."

"How about coming with me tomorrow?"

"You're going to do it again?"

"I don't have anything to do except go to Mass and hang around. I might as well spread the word."

"You're really hung up on this thing, aren't you?"

Espie reminded her about Mark, and Teresa asked, "What Mass do you go to?"

"Eight o'clock."

"I'll meet you here at nine thirty, okay?"

"Make it ten. We have menudo after church," Espie said.

When they met the next morning Espie asked, "You going to wear that wig until your hair grows in?"

"I tried not to wear it this morning, but I feel . . ." Teresa shrugged. "I feel like a freak. You know what I mean."

Espie pushed her hair back into place. "Yeah, I know."

Teresa said, "I told my parents last night that Raul had cut my hair with a knife."

"Your father ready to kill him?"

"He didn't believe me. Neither did my mother."

Espie stared at her. "Who do they think did it?"

"They said I probably did it myself."

"Why?"

"Because I wanted to break up with Raul."

"Did you tell them they were crazy?" Teresa looked away and Espie knew Teresa would never say that to her parents.

They passed people on their way to ten-thirty Mass. "Don't they think he's too old for you?" Espie asked.

"He's thirty-six. That's how old my father was when he married my mother. She turned sixteen the day before they were married. They think it's great an older man likes me so much."

"When is Raul coming back from Tijuana?" Espie asked.

"I don't know. Sometimes he goes early Saturday and comes back the same day. Sometimes he gets back on Sunday. Sometimes he doesn't come home until Monday. I guess it depends on how long it takes him to give the food and clothes to people who need it the most. I don't know. He doesn't talk much about what he does."

"Where does he get the stuff?"

"He asks around for it and people give it to him."

Espie remembered Raul's silk flowered shirt and the spotless white pants. "Does he have a regular job?"

"He makes tables and chairs. Nice ones. I guess that's how he gets his money," Teresa said.

They approached a small grocery store that shaded three men in front of it. The men elbowed each other and whistled between their teeth. "Pretty girls. Pretty girls. I love you. Make love to me," they said. Espie put her thumbs in the belt loops of her jeans and strolled past them. They sounded like Spanish parrots.

Teresa said, "Stupid TJs."

"Hey, that's our people you're talking about," Espie told her.

"I hate wetbacks. They make Anglos think Mexicans are dirty and lazy." The whistles faded behind them. "Raul says the police should round up all the wetbacks in L.A. and ship them back to Tijuana."

"They can't. Thousands of them have crossed the border."

"I know. There's a couple of them on our street. But they work. They don't sit in the shade all day and undress girls with their eyes." Teresa stopped. "Hey, you're not going to tell the police I know a couple of wetbacks, are you?"

Espie faced Teresa. "I told you that uniform doesn't make me a fink."

Teresa started up the walk to a house. "Sorry," she said.

Espie knocked on the door and a woman answered. When Espie told her about the danger of doors on abandoned refrigerators, the woman said, "There is one in the back yard."

Laughter and giggles came from around the house. Espie and Teresa hurried over the weed-covered grass and the woman followed them. Four children pushed wheeless toy cars through the dirt. Espie went to the scarred, dented refrigerator. Her hand shook as she opened the door.

The refrigerator was empty even of shelves. "This door has to come off," she said. She looked at the screws. They'd need a special tool. "Can your husband do it?"

"My husband . . ." The woman shrugged. "He is gone."

Espie glanced at the children, all under eight. "Maybe we can turn it around so the door is against the wall," she said.

She tugged at the refrigerator and Teresa and the woman helped her. It moved a little and they kept pushing and pulling until they had the front of the refrigerator against the house.

Espie asked, "Do you have a refrigerator that works?"

The woman smiled. "My friend, he helped me get one cheap. Ten dollars."

When Espie reached the front of the house, she told Teresa, "Raul doesn't have to go to Tijuana to help the poor. There's plenty of them right here."

"Have you been to TJ?"

"No, my father was going to take me once but . . . he went away before we had a chance to go."

"You have to see the shacks and huts outside Tijuana to know how poor most of the people are." Teresa turned a corner. "Let's do the houses down here. It's on the way to my house and my mother said to bring you for lunch today."

When Teresa introduced Espie to Mr. Hernandez, he looked at her curiously. "I know you. Don't I know you?"

"She was at the police station Tuesday," Teresa said.

Mrs. Hernandez gasped. "You know? You know the terrible thing Teresa did?"

Espie started to defend Teresa. "It's not so ter . . ."

Teresa said, "Espie's not going to tell anybody."

Mr. Hernandez played with the gold band on his finger. "I'm sorry I got so mad. I almost hit you, didn't I?" He looked like a man who was used to apologizing for his temper.

"You were worried," Espie said.

Teresa asked, "Can we eat now? We're going to see more people this afternoon."

Mrs. Hernandez hurried to the kitchen. Her dress looked too big for her the way her sweater had been Tuesday night. "I made chicken salad sandwiches. Is that all right?" she asked, looking at Espie.

Espie followed her. "I love them," she said.

Mrs. Hernandez asked, "You won't tell anybody about Teresa, will you?" Espie took a bite of her sandwich and felt as though the food was a bribe.

She had started her second sandwich when the door swung open and Raul strolled in, dressed in light-blue pants and a pink shirt. "Hey, just in time for lunch," he said without a knock or even a hello.

Mrs. Hernandez jumped to her feet. "Raul, come sit down with us. I'll make a sandwich for you."

"Make it about three. I haven't eaten since breakfast in TJ."

Espie felt like an outsider until she realized he hadn't even looked at Teresa.

Mr. Hernandez said, "How was the trip?"

"Terrific. Always terrific," Raul said. He tilted his chair back and looked at Espie. "Hey, aren't you the mini-pig who was here yesterday?"

Teresa moved forward as if to say something, then leaned back without talking. Espie said, "It's Espie, in case you ever want to talk to me again."

Raul's mouth smiled, but his eyes were angry. "Espie? That's short for Esperanza, isn't it?" Espie nodded. He brought his chair down. "I think I'll call you Esperanza."

Espie stood up and put her thumbs in the belt loops of her jeans. "I like Espie better."

Mrs. Hernandez put the sandwiches in front of Raul. He picked one up. "Well, I'll call you Esperanza. It means hope and I'll hope you don't become a maxi-pig."

Espie asked Teresa, "You coming with me?"

Raul asked, "Where you going?"

Teresa said, "I've been helping her with an Explorer project."

Raul patted the chair beside him. "The only project you have today is to sit here with me."

Teresa sat down and Espie walked to the door. She wasn't going to say good-bye, but before she slammed the door behind her, she turned and waved so Teresa would know she had a friend.

Chapter 6

Espie wanted to call Teresa Sunday night while Mrs.
Garcia and Denise recited the rosary, but she decided
Raul would still be at the Hernandez house. But Monday
night she looked up the number in the phone book and
dialed it. A man said hello and Espie hung up. She recognized Raul's voice and she didn't want to tangle with him
again.

Teresa called Tuesday night. "Can I still go with you to
County General Thursday?"

"Sure, but what about Raul?"

"I told you he goes out with his friends Thursday
nights."

"Won't he find out you were with the mini-pig?" Espie
was sorry as soon as she'd said the words.

"I feel terrible about Sunday," Teresa said.

"What are you going to do about him?"

"I don't know. He just decided I was going to be his girl
and my parents think it's great."

Espie knew Teresa wouldn't be talking the way she was
if anybody was in the house. "Where's everybody tonight?"

Raul took my mother and father someplace to show them a house he wants to buy. There wasn't enough room in the truck, so Raul said I could stay home and do homework."

Espie's temper flared. "Why don't you tell the bastard to go to hell?" she asked.

"I'm afraid of him," Teresa whispered.

Mrs. Garcia's quiet Hail Mary came from the bedroom and Denise answered the prayer. Espie calmed down. "I don't blame you. He sounds like a fruitcake to me."

"Espie, what am I going to do?"

Teresa's voice sounded so desperate, Espie asked, "Why don't you tell the police about Tuesday night?"

"Why should they believe me when my parents don't? I tried to tell them yesterday how afraid I am of Raul and they said I was making it up."

"Why would you?"

"They said so I could go with some Avenue gang. They're so afraid I'm going to get in trouble, they let Raul own me."

"I'll call Officer Parks and ask her what to do."

"No. If Raul finds out, he'll kill me." Teresa's voice shook and Espie imagined her friend waiting alone for a killer.

"I won't give her your name. I'll just say it's about a friend of mine."

"She'll know who I am from the police record. How many sixteen-year-old girls get arrested for lifting a wig to cover chopped-off hair?"

"She's in community relations. She won't even know about your arrest."

"You sure?"

"I'll call you back as soon as I talk to her," Espie said,

and hung up before Teresa had a chance to say not to make the call.

Espie dialed the community relations number and prayed Officer Parks would be in her office. "Community Relations, Officer Parks speaking. May I help you?"

"This is Espie Sanchez."

"Hi, Espie, what can I do for you?"

"I want to ask you a question about a friend of mine."

"What's her name?"

"I can't tell you, but she's in trouble and I said I'd ask you what to do."

"I don't know if I can help you, Espie."

"You have to. Her boyfriend beats her up."

"Did she tell her parents?"

"They won't believe the guy's dangerous. They think he's some kind of saint or something."

"What do you want me to do?"

"He used a knife on her. Can't he be locked up for that?"

"If she files a complaint against him we'll lock him up." The officer sighed. "The only trouble with that is the way the law stands now, he'd probably be back on the street in a few hours, madder than ever."

"You mean a killer can go right back out on the street?"

"That depends. What did he do to her with the knife?"

"He chopped off her hair."

"That doesn't make him a killer."

"Does she have to wait until he sticks the knife in her before the police help her?"

Silence came through the line. Finally Parks said, "Sometimes that's the only way we can hold a prisoner. And if he's got a good lawyer, we may not even be able to do that."

"Then the police can't do anything?"

"I didn't say that. I said if your friend files a complaint, we can bring the guy in. But if he's smart he'll be out in a few hours."

"He's smart," Espie said, and hung up. A cop never gave a yes or no answer.

Mrs. Garcia and Denise were almost finished with the rosary when Espie dialed Teresa's number again. She answered it on the first ring. Espie said, "Officer Parks wasn't much help."

Teresa said, "Hi, Louise," and Espie knew Raul was back with Mr. and Mrs. Hernandez.

Espie said, "I can't talk either. Mrs. Garcia and Denise will be in the room any minute. Just stay loose."

Teresa said, "What are you talking about? We don't have a history test tomorrow."

"I mean don't do anything to get Raul mad. We'll work something out. I'll see you around six thirty Thursday. Okay?"

"Okay, if you want to study the Civil War generals, go ahead. I'm going to work on my English report."

Teresa hung up and Espie put down her receiver. Denise asked, "Who are we picking up Thursday night?"

"Teresa. She's coming with us."

Mrs. Garcia smiled. "Teresa go to the hospital? Maybe she become a L.E.E.G. too."

Espie still stood by the phone as though by doing it she was protecting Teresa. Denise said, "We'd better wrap our presents for the kids."

Mrs. Garcia said, "I have paper." She went to her room and brought out five or six pieces. "I iron it and put it away from last year. It is enough?"

Denise took it. "There's plenty," she said.

Espie moved away from the phone and followed Denise

to their room. She got the doll clothes Mrs. Garcia had made from scraps of cloth left over from the sewing she did for customers and began to wrap the slightly wrinkled paper around the dresses and slips.

Denise asked, "What are you getting Mrs. Garcia for Christmas?"

Espie stopped wrapping. She hadn't even thought about giving a present. Christmas had been just another day at her house ever since her father left. "I don't have any money."

"You don't need money. Make something."

"Like what?"

"I don't know. I'm making a votive candle in arts and crafts at school. The one she has in front of St. Martin's statue is almost gone."

Espie began to wrap a pair of doll's jeans. "I don't have anything I can use to make a present with."

"Think. You'll come up with something."

Espie cut the larger pieces of paper and wrapped the clothes in them. By the time she finished, she still hadn't thought of a present for Mrs. Garcia.

She asked Denise, "What do you think I could give her?"

Denise gathered up the packages. "You figure it out. It took me weeks to think of the votive candle."

Espie sat on her bed. She didn't have weeks. Christmas was just thirteen days away.

When Carlos drove up Thursday night, Denise took the presents and Espie carried the box with the Santa Claus suit. "We have to pick up somebody," Espie told Carlos when she opened the car door.

"Who?"

"Teresa Hernandez. She lives about six blocks up Daly." Espie sat down in the back seat. "I would have called to tell you, but you're always in school or at the taco stand."

Carlos pulled away from the house. "Yeah, well, college is next year. The Explorers are giving me a scholarship, but it doesn't pay for everything."

Espie knew Carlos was going to take police science at Cal State. With his Explorer training and two years of college, he'd have a great future as a cop. She didn't think much about her future. What was there? A job in a store? A waitress? A sewing shop? She told Carlos to turn the corner. "It's the pink house," she said.

Teresa came out as soon as the car stopped. She wore heels, stockings, and a green dress trimmed with red velvet. "My mother said it looked Christmasy," Teresa said. Her voice asked for acceptance.

"The kids will love it," Espie told her, and introduced her to Carlos.

Teresa saw the presents. "I didn't bring anything."

Denise said, "That's okay. We have plenty."

They drove up Figueroa and turned left on York. "What time will you be back at the station?" Carlos asked.

Denise said, "I don't know. Can you wait for us if we're late?"

"Yeah, but I hope it's not too late. I have an algebra test tomorrow."

Denise said, "I'll check with Officer Parks. Maybe she can give us a ride home."

He stopped in the lot by the police station and they walked up the front steps. The policeman on duty outside the door told Espie, "I'll have to check the box."

"It's a Santa Claus suit," Espie said.

"It's a Santa Claus suit to you, but it could be a bomb to me."

Carlos said, "They have to check, Espie."

She opened the box. "Santa won't bring you anything for Christmas," she said.

The officer smiled and picked up the suit to check under it. "Maybe not, but I'll be alive to enjoy the holiday," he said.

When they opened the door, Espie heard laughter from the community-relations office. Denise told Carlos, "I'll go ask Officer Parks about a ride home."

Espie showed Sergeant Jackson the Santa Claus suit. He picked up the beard Mrs. Garcia had made from a piece of felt and some cotton balls and held it up to his chin. "Ho, ho, ho," he said.

"You need a pillow," Espie said.

"So will you," he told her.

"Oh, I'm not going to be Santa Claus."

Denise came back. "Officer Parks said she'd take us home."

"Okay, have fun," Carlos said, and headed for the roll-call room.

When they got to the community-relations room Espie introduced Teresa, and Parks looked at Teresa's hair. Espie knew the officer was wondering if Teresa was the girl Espie had called about.

Alice Eliott took the box from Espie. "This the Santa Claus suit?"

"I hope you brought a pillow," Espie said.

"I brought two just in case," Alice said. She took off her skirt. Espie looked enviously at the lace around the bottom of Alice's slip. Mrs. Garcia had made the one Espie wore under her uniform from a piece of cotton she'd bought at a rummage sale.

Alice pulled on the red pants and Mary Parks helped

her fasten one of the pillows around her waist. Alice put on the red top and tied the beard on. "How do I look?" she asked.

Espie said, "What are you going to do with your hair?"

Mary Parks said, "Here, I have some bobby pins. We can pin it up under the cap."

More girls came in and put their presents in the pillow-case somebody had remembered to bring. Teresa watched the activity without a word. A pounding noise came from the heating pipes. Parks said, "Hey, hold it down. The prisoners are getting excited upstairs."

Roxanne asked, "What do you think they're trying to tell us?"

Espie said, "If you have to ask, you're not ready to know."

The other girls laughed. So did Teresa, and Espie realized it was the first time she had heard her laugh. Officer Parks said, "I told you to hold it down."

Espie, Teresa, and Denise piled into Mary Parks's station wagon with six other girls. Five girls got in Alice's car. Officer Parks told her, "I'd like to see a cop stop you in that outfit."

Alice squeezed in behind the steering wheel. "I can hardly reach the ignition," she said.

Mary Parks laughed and got in her car. "You'll be well padded if you get in an accident," she told Alice.

Espie started to sing "Jingle Bells" as they drove away from the police station. Everybody joined in, but Mary Parks told them to quiet down when she eased her way into the Golden State Freeway traffic.

"You'll have a chance to sing your lungs off at the hospital," she said.

They took the Mission Road turnoff and approached the gate that made the long, high buildings behind it look like a prison. Espie had passed the hospital a few times and each time had prayed she'd never get sick enough to go there.

But Mary Parks didn't go up the hill to the large buildings. She turned left and stopped beside a small, low one surrounded by grass and trees.

After they got out of the station wagon, Teresa whispered, "Officer Parks is nice, isn't she?"

Espie nodded "She's mostly okay."

Teresa straightened her dress. "Who are the other girls without uniforms?"

"They're recruits. They come to meetings and things to see if they want to go through the police academy training to become Explorers." Espie nudged Teresa. "Hey, maybe you'll decide to join."

Teresa said, "Raul wouldn't let me."

Alice drove up with the other Explorers, and Mary Parks strolled to her with the rest of the girls. Espie held back and told Teresa, "You're going to have to do something about that old dude."

"I'm going to kill him," Teresa said.

Espie stared at her. Denise called, "Hey, hurry up, you two," and Espie didn't have a chance to ask Teresa how serious she was.

Chapter 7

Espie was the last one in the hospital reception room. Two small girls raced in their wheelchairs toward Santa Claus. A little boy peeked around his mother's knees at the stranger in red. And a woman with a Red Cross patch on her sleeve hung candy canes on the biggest Christmas tree Espie had ever seen.

Alice turned to the L.E.E.G.s around her. "Ho, ho, ho, do we have presents for these good little girls?" She leaned toward the children. "You *have* been good, haven't you?" The girls nodded while their eyes watched Denise, who brought out two presents and handed them to the girls.

"Can we open them now?" one of them asked.

Alice said, "Of course. It's almost Christmas, isn't it?"

The girls tore off the wrapping paper. One got a puzzle and the other received a coloring book and a box of crayons. The girl with the puzzle said, "I'll let you make my puzzle if you let me color one of the pictures in your book."

The child said okay, and in a moment the puzzle pieces, the crayons, and the book were scattered around the floor.

Espie looked for Teresa. She was on her knees making

friends with the boy who had come out from behind his mother, but who still clung to her dress. Teresa gave no hint of the anger reflected on her face when she said she was going to kill Raul. Espie walked with the rest of the group toward the little boy and decided Teresa hadn't meant what she said. And yet . . .

A woman approached the group. "I'm Mrs. Zarcoff. I'll be your guide. But before we go upstairs there're a few rules I have to ask you to obey. The first one is that you can't give food to the children in Rooms 35 and 36. They're on special diets, so if you have candy or cake, don't bring them in these rooms. Another thing—nobody goes into the intensive care unit. Most of the kids in there are so sick they wouldn't know you were there anyway, and we don't want to take the chance of bringing more germs to patients already in a life or death situation. You may sing carols and distribute your gifts, but no running around or loud talking. Remember, this is a hospital." The woman turned. "Come with me," she said.

Alice and the others followed until Espie said, "Hey, how about a present for this kid?"

Mrs. Zarcoff said, "I told you no loud talking." Alice pushed the pillow up under the Santa Claus suit and took the present Denise handed her. Alice gave it to the boy with her ho, ho, ho, and Mrs. Zarcoff rushed everybody onto the elevator before the child unwrapped the present.

After Mrs. Zarcoff's speech, Espie was sure the place would be a downer. But when the elevator doors opened, she saw pictures of cartoon characters on the walls behind children who laughed and talked while they walked around or sat in wheelchairs. Nurses in bright uniforms pushed carts with trays of medicines. And two men beside a desk examined a chart.

Everybody stopped what they were doing and looked at

Santa Claus and his Explorers, who were immediately surrounded by kids. Officer Parks began to sing "Jingle Bells" and everybody joined in. When they finished, the adults went back to what they'd been doing, but the kids grabbed the presents and candy the Explorers passed out. Within minutes, papers and toys covered the floor.

Mrs. Zarcoff ignored the mess. "Follow me to the rooms," she said.

There were four beds in each room. Only half the Explorers could squeeze in at one time, so while one group was in one room with Alice, the other group went in another room to talk to the kids and tell them Santa Claus was coming with presents.

There was so much going on, Espie didn't have a chance to talk to Teresa, but she seemed to be enjoying herself, and Espie decided to forget what Teresa had said about Raul.

None of the kids looked very sick and Espie wondered why they were in the hospital. Doctors and nurses came in and out of rooms. They looked busy, but they teased and laughed with the patients and the L.E.E.G.s.

After all the kids in that section had received presents and candy, Mrs. Zarcoff led the girls down another hall. Officer Parks said, "Let's sing 'Santa Claus Is Coming to Town' so they'll know we're on our way."

They had finished the second line of the song when they passed a closed door marked INTENSIVE CARE UNIT. Espie stood on her toes to look in the window in the door. Suddenly, it opened, and a woman no taller than Espie almost knocked her over. "Oh, excuse me," the woman said. "I just wanted to see what was happening." Her black hair was pinned above the collar of her yellow jacket.

"We're giving presents to the kids," Espie told her. The rest of the group had moved down the hall. Espie looked past the woman. There were six cribs in the room. One of them was covered with plastic. "What's that?" she asked the woman.

"It's an oxygen tent. Jordan's a very sick boy."

"Is he going to die?" Espie asked.

"Not if I can help it."

Espie glanced at the woman's name tag—Dr. Martinez. "You're a doctor?" she asked. The woman nodded. "I've never seen a woman doctor before. I mean, you know, I've never even seen many doctors."

The woman laughed. She hadn't left her place by the door where she could watch the small patients inside. "Well, there aren't as many women doctors as there should be, but we're gaining."

Roxanne hurried up the hall. "Officer Parks said to stay with the group."

"Okay, I'm coming," Espie said. She turned toward Dr. Martinez. "Is it hard being a doctor? I mean is it hard to become a doctor?"

"It's hard, but it's worth it."

"Doesn't the job scare you?"

Dr. Martinez nodded and looked at her patients. "Especially in this ward," she said.

Roxanne pulled at Espie's arm and Espie followed her. "Thanks," she said to Dr. Martinez.

When Espie reached the other girls, Denise was on the floor helping a small boy unwrap a present. Espie asked, "Where's Teresa?"

Denise looked around. "I don't know. She was here a couple of minutes ago." A group of visitors had gathered around the laughing children.

A short, husky man called out, "Save one for my son. He's down the hall." The man's arms bulged beneath his red shirt.

Officer Parks said, "We have enough. This is our last group."

Mrs. Zarcoff said, "And visiting hours are almost finished."

Espie glanced in the room beside her. The four beds were empty and Teresa was just inside the door, her body tight against the wall.

"What are you doing in here?" she asked.

"That man, the short one with the red shirt, that's one of the guys Raul shoots pool with."

"So why don't you go out and talk to him?"

"I don't want Raul to know I came."

Two children came in the room with their presents, and the Explorer group moved down the hall with Santa Claus. Espie said, "I have to go. Talk to the kids. If anybody asks what you're doing here, tell them you're visiting your cousin."

"What will Officer Parks say?"

"If she misses you, I'll tell her you're visiting one of your cousins and we'll pick you up on the way down the hall."

The children were asking questions and their voices grew louder when Espie and Teresa didn't answer. Finally, Teresa moved away from the wall and led one of the small girls to her bed. "I'm your cousin Teresa," she said.

The little girl said, "You don't look like my cousin Teresa. My cousin Teresa is fat and tall and dresses funny."

Teresa helped the child into bed. "I'm your other cousin Teresa," she said.

Espie laughed. "Don't forget to get in the group when we pass the room on the way back."

"I won't," Teresa said.

The son of Raul's friend lay unmoving when the Explorers went in his room to tell him and the other children Santa Claus was coming. The man said to Espie, "I've already told him he was going to get a present."

Espie went to stand beside the bed. The boy smiled, but he still didn't move, and Espie realized he couldn't. "What's your name?" she asked.

"Bobby."

"What happened to you, Bobby?" she asked. The L.E.E.G.s in the room laughed and talked to the children in the other three beds.

"Some guys beat me up," the boy said.

He looked so small under the sheet, Espie asked, "How old are you?"

"Eight."

The boy's father swore. "Eight years old and he won't walk again. For a quarter. For a goddam quarter." He hit the wall with his fist. "I'll kill them. If I find them, I'll kill them."

Everyone turned and stared at him. At that moment, Alice came in with her ho, ho, ho, and the children giggled. Alice didn't look like the Santa Claus who had left the Northeast Division Police Station. Strands of hair hung below the red hat, the pillow had slipped so far inside the Santa Claus pants she could hardly walk. But she was still smiling.

Espie took the present someone gave her and asked the boy if he wanted her to open it for him. He told her yes. She tore off the paper and held up a fire truck. She started to hand it to him, then realized he couldn't take it. "Where do you want me to put it?" she asked.

"On my belly."

Espie put the toy on Bobby's chest. "Hey, when I breathe the truck moves up and down and when I blink it looks like it's moving."

Mrs. Zarcoff told the girls, "You'll have to go now. Visiting hours are over." She looked at Bobby's father. "You can stay a few minutes longer," she said.

When Espie left the room, the man was pushing the truck on Bobby's stomach, the boy was laughing, and Espie was crying.

She brushed away the tears with the back of her hand. The activity in the halls hadn't slowed down. The L.E.E.G.s passed the room Teresa was in and she joined the group. "Any trouble?" Espie whispered.

"No," Teresa said, and moved into the center of the group. They passed the intensive care unit. Dr. Martinez didn't come out. Espie wondered how the boy in the oxygen tent was doing. It must be terrible to know a person's life depends on you, Espie thought.

She had tried to save Mark and couldn't. Could she save anybody? Maybe. After all, Mark had been dead too long for her to help him. She shivered when she remembered his cold mouth on hers. Maybe I could be a nurse, Espie thought. That's crazy, she told herself immediately. They got on the elevator, the door closed, and they started down. Yeah, that's crazy, she told herself again.

By the time they reached the lobby, Alice's Santa Claus pants had fallen down and Espie was laughing with everybody else. The pillow tumbled to the floor. Alice sat on it and laughed until tears rolled down her cheeks. The lobby was empty except for a switchboard operator who stared at the giggling girls.

"That was fun," Alice said. Then she stopped laughing. "Except it was sad, too."

She stood up, picked up the pillow and the pants from

the Santa Claus suit, and walked to the car in her slip. It was the first time Espie had seen Alice lose her cool, and Espie liked her a little bit better because of it.

The girls split up in two groups. Mary Parks took the ones who lived east of Figueroa Street and Alice took the ones who lived west of it.

No one sang. Instead, they talked about what the kids had said to them and the way their faces glowed when they opened the presents. Alice was right. It had been fun, but it had been sad, too.

Mary Parks dropped off each girl in front of her house until only Espie, Denise, and Teresa were left. Teresa told the officer how to get to the Hernandez house and Mary Parks asked, "Did you enjoy yourself, Teresa?"

"Yes, I did," Teresa told her.

"Maybe you'll decide to join the group."

Teresa said, "I don't know. I'm pretty busy."

They turned the corner to her house. Teresa stiffened. Raul's truck was parked in front of her house. When Officer Parks stopped the station wagon, Teresa opened the car door. "Thank you for taking me," she said, and her voice sounded so strange that if Espie hadn't seen Teresa say the words, Espie wouldn't have believed her friend was talking.

Mary Parks waited to make sure Teresa was safely on her front porch before she drove off. But Teresa didn't need protection outside. She needed it inside.

When they reached Mrs. Garcia's house, Denise hopped out. "Thanks for the ride. I'll see you tomorrow night at the Christmas tree lot," she said.

Espie was halfway out the door when Officer Parks said, "Teresa is the girl you called me about, isn't she?"

Espie's hand froze to the door. "That's crazy. Does Teresa's hair look like it's been chopped off with a knife?"

"She has a wig on," Mary Parks said. "And she was hiding from somebody at the hospital."

"How did you know?"

"A police officer is trained to observe. Maybe we'll have a lesson on that during the meeting next week."

"Yeah, well, I have to go," Espie said, moving away from the door.

"If you need me, Espie, you know how to get in touch with me."

"Yeah," Espie said, and closed the door.

Denise was already in her pajamas by the time Espie got in. "Hurry and put the lights out, will you? I'm really tired."

Espie got her pajamas and put out the light. "I'll change in the bathroom," she said.

She put her things on the chair near the phone and picked up the receiver. She dialed three numbers before she hung it up again.

Teresa was safe. Raul wouldn't slap her around if her parents were there. Espie put on her pajamas and went to brush her teeth. She hurried back to the phone. Suppose her parents weren't home? She reached for the phone and jumped when it rang.

She grabbed it. "Hello."

Teresa said, "Espie, guess what?" Teresa sounded so happy, Espie thought Raul had left her because she had gone out. "Raul is going to Tijuana next weekend with more presents and he wants me to go with him. And he wants you to come, too."

Espie almost dropped the phone. "Me? Why does he want me to go to Mexico with him?"

"He said now that he knows I'm interested in doing charity work I can help him with his and he wants you to

60

help, too. He said we can go down Saturday morning and come back Saturday night."

A man's voice came over the phone. "That's right, Esperanza. You come with me. I'll show you what it's like to really help people."

Espie finally found her voice. "I'll have to ask Mrs. Garcia."

"Okay, ask her."

"She's sleeping."

"Well, you ask her tomorrow, but she'll say yes when she knows why you're going."

"Okay, Raul."

Espie put down the receiver and sat on the chair near the phone. A chance to go to Tijuana! Raul was right. Mrs. Garcia would say Espie could go. Or would she? She was always preaching about the terrible things that happened to girls. Espie and Denise were only allowed out of the house when they were with Mrs. Garcia or on Explorer business.

Espie wondered why Raul wanted her with him. She stared at the phone. She should call him and tell him she wouldn't go. She reached for it, then stood up and walked to the bathroom. She couldn't call him. It didn't matter why he wanted her. She wanted to go to Mexico and this was her chance.

Chapter 8

As soon as Mrs. Garcia woke Denise and Espie the next morning, Espie asked if she could go to Tijuana with Teresa and her boyfriend.

Mrs. Garcia gasped. "What kind of parents Teresa have they let her go to Mexico with her boyfriend?"

Espie pushed back the blankets. "They'll only be gone for the day. Raul is taking more stuff to give to the poor for Christmas."

"Raul? What is his last name?" Mrs. Garcia looked interested.

"Torres," Espie said.

Mrs. Garcia smiled. "Teresa's boyfriend is Raul Torres? She is lucky to have such a nice boy."

Denise went to the bathroom and Espie began to dress. "You know him?" she asked.

"The ladies in the altar society talk about the nice things he do." Mrs. Garcia started out of the room. "I must watch the breakfast," she said.

Espie followed her. "Can I go with them?" she asked.

Mrs. Garcia frowned. "You go in the morning and come back at night?" Espie nodded. The woman turned over the eggs. "I think you can go. You will be safe with Raul."

Espie gave a cheer that brought Denise from the bathroom. "What's going on?"

Espie ran past her to the bedroom. "I'm going to Mexico," she called back.

As soon as she reached the bedroom she turned around and ran to the phone. "I have to call Teresa." She dialed and Teresa answered on the third ring. "I can go with you," Espie told her.

"Great. I'll tell Raul this afternoon. He really wants you to come with us."

"Why?"

"I don't know. He just said he wants you to come. You know, I think he really likes you."

"Maybe," Espie said. She wondered if she could be wrong about Raul. After all, Teresa's parents thought he was great. Mrs. Garcia and the altar society ladies thought so too. And he *did* help a lot of people. "I'll talk to you later," she told Teresa, and hung up. Espie began to eat. She couldn't believe she was wrong. Raul wanted her with him only because she could help in some way, and she wished she knew what it was.

Mrs. Garcia put buttered toast on the table. "If Officer Parks asks you to work the desk or sell Christmas trees Sunday, tell her we go to Olvera Street for *las posadas*," she told Espie and Denise.

Espie said, "I love Olvera Street."

Mrs. Garcia asked, "You go many times?"

"Just once with my father. He said he'd bring me again, but . . ." Espie went back to eating. She didn't have to explain her father had left the family before he had a chance to take her back to the block-long cobblestone street lined with Mexican shops in the center of Los Angeles.

Denise asked Espie, "Did he take you to *las posadas*?"

Espie shook her head. "We just went down there one Sunday. The place was crawling with tourists."

"That was nothing compared to what goes on at Christmas. Thousands of people squeeze into that street for the yearly crunch."

Mrs. Garcia said, "The people who are Mary and Joseph have trouble getting to the doors of the shops to ask for a room."

Espie's grandmother had told her almost every Christmas how the people in her Mexican village began the Christmas season on December 16 with people going from house to house to ask for a place to stay the way Mary and Joseph had done in Bethlehem thousands of years ago. Espie had always wanted to see the ceremony.

She brought her empty plate to the sink. "Do they sing and carry candles and everything?" she asked.

Mrs. Garcia said, "On Olvera Street, they do like in Mexico."

Espie smiled. "Hey, how about that? It's only seven thirty and already I'm going to Tijuana and Olvera Street. By tonight I may be going to the moon."

Denise laughed. "Would you settle for the Christmas tree lot? We can use extra help on Friday nights."

"Maybe I'll go with you," Espie said, and went to finish getting dressed.

She had to undress again an hour later for P.E. She hated having physical education first period. It was always freezing. Even when the temperature went up to seventy or eighty during the day, it was usually around fifty-five degrees at eight thirty. And the stupid teacher insisted they change to gym shorts and a short-sleeved blouse. "Come on, let's get out there and get the blood circulating," she yelled at the girls in different stages of undress.

Espie pulled on her shorts. "What does she think my blood's doing now?" she said to no one in particular.

She got on the playing field for softball. Four minutes after the game started she was on her way to the health office with a hurt index finger. "What happened?" the nurse, Mrs. Harrington, asked.

"I tried to stop a grounder." The nurse looked at the finger and moved it around. Espie winced.

"It doesn't seem broken," the woman said.

"It hurts."

Mrs. Harrington reached for an ice bag. "Here, hold this on it."

A guy came in with a bloody nose. The nurse made him sit with his head back. "Hold this ice on the back of your neck," she said.

Espie asked, "Do you take care of everything with ice?"

Mrs. Harrington chuckled. "It seems like it around here."

Espie took off the ice and tried to bend her finger. She put the ice back. "You like being a nurse?"

"Very much," Mrs. Harrington said.

"I met a woman doctor last night. She's Mexican."

"She must be an unusual person."

Espie sat straighter in her chair. "Don't you think Mexicans can be doctors?"

"Sure they can. But it's harder for them."

"Why?"

"Not enough education. Not enough money. I think a woman who becomes a doctor is special. But if she's Mexican or black she has to work twice as hard, and sometimes be twice as smart as a man."

The boy with the bloody nose asked, "Hey, how long do I have to sit here and listen to this woman's liberation junk?"

Mrs. Harrington checked him. "You can go, but stay away from the other guy's fist for a while," she said. She took the ice off Espie's finger. "How does it feel?" Espie bent it and winced. "I'll put a small splint on it. It'll be okay." Mrs. Harrington put what looked like two wide popsicle sticks on the finger. It really didn't hurt much. But Espie decided to fake it and get the splint so she could get out of writing during her classes. It was the third nice thing to happen to her that day.

While the other kids wrote assignments, Espie thought about what the nurse had said. Espie knew little about nurses and doctors. She remembered seeing a doctor once when she was small. Then when she joined the Explorer program, a doctor had examined her to make sure she could make it through the training. Until she took first aid at the Academy, she had no idea how to move an injured person, stop a bleeding wound, or give mouth-to-mouth resuscitation like she had tried to give Mark.

First aid had been her favorite class at the Academy, and she thought a couple of times then about being a nurse. But she had decided the idea was silly. She thought that last night, too. But now, while the kids struggled with a history test, Espie wondered who she could ask for information without being laughed at. She decided to ask Officer Parks.

On the way home Espie took off the splint and threw it in the wire trash basket on the corner of Daly and Broadway. There was nothing really wrong with the finger, and if Mrs. Garcia saw the splint she wouldn't let Espie go sell Christmas trees, and she was anxious to talk to Mary Parks.

Carlos picked up Espie and Denise at six thirty. "I didn't know you were on duty tonight," he said to Espie when she got in the car with Denise.

"I just decided to go along to help. Denise said Friday nights are busy."

"Yeah, most people get paid and a lot of them come buy their tree."

Denise started to tell Carlos about the visit to the hospital and they talked about the kids during most of the ride. When Carlos parked by the police station, Espie realized she hadn't felt as excited about riding with him as she usually did. One of the reasons she had joined the Explorers was so she could be with him, but it looked like he just wanted to be friends with her the way he was friends with Denise. And as they walked to the Christmas tree lot, Espie was surprised to find that that was the way she felt, too. He was "going steady" with the Explorers and his work because it would lead to a good future, and Espie decided she wouldn't break up the romance even if she could. Besides, now that she had an idea about her future, she understood how he felt.

Mary Parks smiled when she saw them. "Hi," she said to Denise and Carlos. She turned to Espie. "I'm glad you came."

Espie said, "Yeah, well, I thought you could use some help."

"We always need that. But we won't be too rushed tonight. A few extra boys showed up."

Denise and Carlos walked over to a couple of customers. Espie asked Officer Parks, "What do I do?"

"When a customer comes in, ask him what size tree he's looking for. You know, give everybody a smile and be friendly. A lot of them will try to talk the price down. Tell them our trees are already priced lower than anybody else around so we can't lower them any more."

"Are they?" Espie asked.

"Are they what?"

"Are they priced lower than anybody else around?"

Parks laughed. "Espie, you're a skeptic."

"What's that?"

"A skeptic is a person who doesn't believe everything he hears or sees."

"I don't call that being skeptic. I call that being smart."

Mary Parks strolled toward a customer and Espie followed her. The officer said, "I knew you were smart when I talked to you the first night the police brought you in for running away from home."

Only two other people had told Espie she was smart— her grandmother and Mrs. Garcia. "Thanks," Espie said.

A woman entered the tree lot and Espie went to her. "What size tree do you want?" she asked.

The woman shrugged. "I'm just looking tonight. My husband gets paid tomorrow and I want to see how much the trees are this year."

Espie glanced at the tag on the tree. "Ten dollars!" she said before she could stop herself.

The woman said, "Oh, that's too much." They moved toward smaller trees. Espie held up a skinny one with two broken branches. The woman looked at the tag. "It's five dollars," she said.

Espie told her, "Let me check on it. Somebody must have made a mistake."

The woman shook her head. "I'm sure it's right. The price of trees goes higher and higher every year. I told my husband we might not be able to afford one this time, but he said the kids had to have a tree." The woman smiled. "Thank you," she said. "Maybe I'll come back tomorrow." Espie remembered how much she had enjoyed the trees her family had while her father was home and hoped the woman would come back.

A man entered the lot, looked around, and hurried to

the largest trees. He was holding one away from him by the time she reached him. "Here, hold this so I can get a better look at it," he said.

Espie grabbed the tree as he let it go and it almost knocked her over. She glanced at the price tag. "This tree costs thirty dollars," she said.

"I'll take it," the man said.

"It's thirty dollars," Espie said again because she thought he hadn't heard her.

He took three ten-dollar bills and a couple of ones from his pocket. "Here you go. That should cover the tax," he said, and gave the money to Espie. He put out his hand and Espie let go of the tree. "Thanks," he said. "The kids will have lots of fun trimming this."

Espie watched him struggle to get it into his station wagon. She wished the woman before him could have only a small piece of that tree.

She brought the money to Parks. "That's some sale," the officer said.

"The guy didn't look like he was hurting for money." She shivered.

Mary Parks said, "You must be freezing with only that sweater on. Let's go to my office. I brought hot chocolate."

Espie hugged herself. "You don't use a coat much in Los Angeles, but when you need one, you really need one."

They entered the building. Mary Parks asked, "Doesn't Mrs. Garcia have a coat left by any of the girls she took care of?"

Espie shook her head. "She was going to buy me one last month, but the landlord raised the rent. He said he had to. The taxes were killing him."

"She can get the money from the people downtown."

"Yeah, but she says other people need the money more than she does. She won't even sign up for the free lunch program at school. She says she can sew to make a little money, but some people don't make anything, so they should get the money."

Parks poured the hot chocolate. "But the money belongs to her. I'll talk to her."

"She said she'd try to get me a coat in a couple of weeks." Espie took a sip from her cup. "Did you mean it when you said I was smart?" she asked.

"Of course I did."

"Smart enough to be a nurse?"

Mary Parks looked up. "You going to be a nurse?"

Espie looked down at her cup. "I've been thinking about it."

"That's great, Espie."

"What do I have to do? I mean, what kind of school would I go to?"

"There're a lot of good nursing schools around."

"How tough are they?"

"I don't think you'd have any problem getting through."

Espie took another sip of her hot chocolate. Steam escaped from the radiators and she began to feel warm. "I only have a C average."

Mary Parks sat down. "I know. And your counselor told me you could do better."

"No way."

"How long do you study at night?"

Espie shrugged and took another sip of chocolate. "I do my homework."

"If you get a C average with just doing your homework, you'd have no problem getting a B with a little bit of studying. And if you're going to be a nurse, you'd better get used to studying."

"It's that tough, huh?"

Mary Parks sighed. "Espie, you can't just slide through school. It's like everything else. If you're going to succeed, you're going to have to work."

Espie didn't want a sermon. "Maybe if they taught something I could use, I'd be more interested."

"You have a new Mexican history study course this year. That's a step up, isn't it?"

"Yeah, but it won't help me become a nurse."

"It'll teach you to be proud you're Mexican."

Espie put down her cup. "I've always been proud I'm Mexican," she said. Mary Parks sipped her chocolate and didn't look away. Espie asked, "Is it expensive? The nursing school, I mean."

"There are ways to get help. The Explorers have a scholarship you can try for. And there're government grants and government loans. It won't be easy, but what is?" Mary Parks leaned forward. "Espie, you can be anything you want to be if you want it badly enough."

They sat in silence. Only the heat passing through the pipes disturbed the quiet. "I guess we'd better get back outside," Espie said. She hated to leave the warmth, but she didn't want any more terrific sayings like, "You can be anything you want to be."

Mary Parks stood up and threw away the paper cups. "I'd like to put some of our profit from this sale in a bank account for a trip to Europe."

"Europe?" Espie stopped in the middle of the hall.

"It would take a long time to save enough from our projects, but other Explorer groups have done it."

Espie laughed and started down the hall again. "What's so funny?" the officer asked.

"When I got up this morning I'd never been anyplace and I wasn't going anyplace. Now I'm going to Olvera

Street Sunday for *las posadas*, to Tijuana next Saturday, and to Europe some day."

"Don't plan on Europe. It's probably just one of my crazy dreams," Mary Parks said. She opened the door. "Who are you going to TJ with?"

"Teresa and her boyfriend, Raul. He's going down there to bring presents and he asked me and Teresa to go."

"Raul? What's his last name?"

"Torres. Do you know him?"

"Not personally. But a lot of people have told me about the nice things he does."

"Everybody thinks he's a great guy," Espie said.

"That's what I hear," Parks said, and walked toward a customer. Espie didn't think she sounded convinced.

Chapter 9

When the mailman came Saturday morning, he left two packages for Mrs. Garcia. "They come. I tell them not to send presents, but they do not listen," Mrs. Garcia said. "And the Christmas cards, they are always so beautiful."

Cards had been arriving at the house for weeks and Mrs. Garcia held about a dozen more that the mailman had handed her with the presents.

Espie knew they were from girls Mrs. Garcia had been foster mother to. Denise asked, "How many girls have you taken care of?"

Mrs. Garcia began to take the paper off one of the presents. "Many. Some stay only a day, some stay weeks, and some stay years until they are eighteen and the law say they are grown up."

She opened the box, took out the pink cloth, and read the note attached to the material. "Make a pretty dress and send me a picture of you wearing it so I can show my children the beautiful woman who gave me love."

Mrs. Garcia blushed. "She always say things like that."

Denise said, "I think that's great. Here, open this one."

Espie didn't know why she felt uncomfortable when people said nice things. Maybe it was because she wasn't used to hearing them.

Mrs. Garcia held up a flowered nightgown. "This is too pretty for me," she said.

Denise told her, "Wow, it looks like a garden. I mean . . ."

Mrs. Garcia laughed. "It is big enough to be a garden," she said, and Espie laughed with her.

Mrs. Garcia put the presents near the couch. "We will put them around the *nacimiento* tomorrow. I always fix the stable on the first day of *las posadas*." She put the Christmas cards on the table. "I will open these later," she said.

That evening, while Mrs. Garcia cooked supper, Espie asked Denise, "Are you finished with Mrs. Garcia's votive candle?"

"I'm leaving it at school until vacation. Have you decided what you're going to give her?"

Espie shook her head. "Can't you think of anything?"

"I've really tried, but I can't come up with anything. Maybe you can give her a present of time or something like that."

"Time?"

"You know. Wrap up a note that reads, 'This entitles you to ten nights off from washing dishes or five weekends of house cleaning.' "

"That's dumb," Espie said.

Denise shrugged and Espie went to call Teresa. Mrs. Hernandez answered. "She's gone with Raul to get presents to bring to Tijuana. She called you to go with them, but nobody was home. Do you want her to call you?"

"Yeah, I'll be home," Espie said, and hung up.

Mrs. Garcia asked, "Teresa is not home?" Espie shook her head. Mrs. Garcia took three plates from the cabinet. "Please tell Denise it is time to eat," she said.

After they finished their burritos and chile, Mrs. Garcia asked Espie and Denise to do the dishes. "I have much sewing. Everybody want the things for Christmas."

She went to the foot-operated sewing machine and Espie said, "You wash, I'll dry."

"I always have to wash," Denise complained.

"That's because you're so good at it," Espie said.

Denise turned on the faucet. "It's because you'll argue until I give in," she said.

When the kitchen had been cleaned up, Denise went back to the bedroom and Espie checked the free TV guide the supermarket gave out. There wasn't anything she wanted to watch. She wished Teresa would call.

She went to the bedroom. "What are you reading?" she asked Denise.

"A story about Helen Keller."

"Who is she?"

Denise put down her book. "A great woman."

"What made her so great?" Espie lay across her bed.

"She lived a full life even though she was handicapped."

"What's a handicap?"

"It's something that makes it hard for a person to do something. Like Helen Keller. She was deaf, blind, and she couldn't talk until she was grown, but it didn't stop her from graduating from college and helping people all over the world."

"How?" Espie asked, and sat up.

Denise laughed. "If you want to know, you'll have to read the book. I hate to tell stories."

75

Espie lay back down. When the clock struck seven, the sewing machine stopped. Denise put down her book and headed toward Mrs. Garcia's room to say the rosary. Denise looked at Espie on the way out to see if she was coming, but she pretended not to see her.

She reached over and picked up the book on Denise's bed. She glanced at a couple of pages. She wasn't much of a reader, but her English teacher gave extra credit for book reports. Maybe she could get a B if she really tried. She rolled over on her stomach and started to read. If Helen Keller had done as many things as Denise said she did, Espie should be able to become a nurse. The only handicap she had to overcome were the screwballs who thought Mexicans were lazier and dumber than paddies.

The phone rang at eight thirty. Mrs. Garcia was back at her sewing machine and Denise was reading the book she had taken back after she finished the rosary. Espie ran to the phone and picked it up on the second ring. "Hello."

Teresa said, "Hi, Espie. I called this afternoon, but you weren't home."

"I know. Your mother told me. Did you get many presents?"

"Stacks of them. Raul knows all the owners of those sewing shops and they gave him a lot of dresses. They're seconds. You know, that means there's something wrong with them, but you can hardly tell. And we got a lot of shoes. And toys. Boxes of toys."

Espie said, "I guess things are okay between you and Raul now."

Silence came from the other end of the line. For a moment Espie thought Raul had been listening. Teresa said finally, "No, that hasn't changed. But can you help us wrap presents Thursday and Friday?" The way Teresa ran the two sentences together Espie knew Raul was with her.

"Wait, I'll ask Mrs. Garcia." Espie put down the phone and went to the sewing machine. Mrs. Garcia looked up. "Teresa wants to know if I can help her and Raul wrap the presents for Tijuana Thursday and Friday."

Mrs. Garcia cut the material loose from the machine. "School ends Wednesday?"

Espie nodded. "Until after New Years."

"That is fine. You can help," the woman said.

Espie hurried back to the phone. "I can do it. We going to wrap at your house?"

"No, everything's at Raul's apartment."

Espie wanted to back down. "Hey, well, listen, I have an Explorer meeting Thursday night."

"That's okay, we'll be working during the day."

"How do I get there?" Espie hoped it would be too far for her to walk.

"We'll pick you up around ten. Raul said he'll fix lunch for us." The person they were talking about didn't sound like the Raul who had cut off his girl's hair so nobody else would want her, or the Raul Teresa said she was going to kill.

"Okay, I'll be ready at ten. You want to come to the L.E.E.G. meeting?"

Espie heard a gasp, then Raul said, "Esperanza, stop asking Teresa to go places with you. She's mine and I say where she can go and where she can't go."

Espie slammed down the phone. *That* was the Raul Teresa said she was going to kill. And Espie didn't want any part of him, not even for a trip to TJ.

Mrs. Garcia asked, "What is wrong?"

"Nothing," Espie said, and switched on the television

even though there wasn't anything she wanted to watch. When she turned it off at ten o'clock, she heard rain on the roof. Mrs. Garcia wouldn't go to Olvera Street in the rain. "Damn," Espie muttered, and stomped to her room. Denise was still reading. Espie undressed and got into bed. "Hurry up and turn off that light," she said, and faced the wall.

Denise asked, "What's *your* problem?"

Espie pulled the blanket over her head and didn't answer.

When Mrs. Garcia woke them up for Mass the next morning, the room was still dark. "It is a bad day for *las posadas*," she said.

Espie got up and raised the shade. "It's only drizzling. We can still go," she said. She thought of how cold it would be in the rain at night with only her sweater, but she didn't care.

Mrs. Garcia said, "Maybe the sun will come later."

She left the room and Denise asked, "What were you so mad about last night?"

"I'm not going to TJ."

"Why not?"

"That Raul is a real nut."

"What's the matter with him?"

Espie shrugged. She couldn't answer without telling her how he treated Teresa. "Do you think we'll go to Olvera Street?"

Denise glanced out the window. "It'll take more than this drizzle to stop Mrs. Garcia from going to *las posadas*." Espie put on her jeans. Denise said, "You know she doesn't like you to wear jeans to church."

"It's this or my dress and my uniform shoes." Espie slipped on her sandals and went to the kitchen. Mrs. Garcia glanced at her clothes, but she didn't say anything.

By the time they came out of church the light rain had stopped, but it was damp and cold. They walked as quickly as Mrs. Garcia could move, and by the time they got home, Espie was frozen.

Mrs. Garcia turned on the small wall heater and gave the menudo pan to Denise. "You go for the menudo. You have a coat," she said.

The threat of rain hung over them until almost four, when the sun shone a few minutes before it disappeared again behind the clouds. Mrs. Garcia said, "I think we go. It will not be Christmas without *las posadas*."

Her words started everybody moving. Denise turned off the old movie she was watching on television, Espie put down the Helen Keller book, and Mrs. Garcia spooned frijoles from the ever-present pot on the back of the stove. She warmed tortillas over the gas flame and put plates on the table. "We will eat now. There will be many people at Olvera Street. Besides . . ." She didn't have to finish. Espie knew there wasn't any money for them to eat at one of the stands that lined the street.

They waited a long time for the bus, but the ride only took a little more than ten minutes. Before Espie saw the steeple of the Church of Our Lady, Queen of the Angels, cars lined the streets and overflowed the parking lots. When she got off the bus with Mrs. Garcia and Denise, they were immediately surrounded by people.

Espie stared around her. "Where'd they all come from?"

Denise laughed. "It's early yet, wait until later."

Christmas carols came from the Plaza. The beat of a mariachi band across the street almost drowned out "Silent Night."

Mrs. Garcia said, "We go see the *nacimiento*."

Espie wanted to get on Olvera Street, not see a stable, but she made her way through the crowd to the Plaza, with Mrs. Garcia leading the way.

Espie said, "Hey, the hedges are shaped like animals. There's a giraffe. And there's a bear."

Denise asked, "Didn't you see them when you came with your father?"

Espie shook her head. "How do they get that way?"

"A gardener trims them into shape. There's one that looks like a lion."

Espie stopped moving and stood on her tiptoes, but she couldn't see it over everybody's heads. "Let's walk around and see them all," she said.

They were almost at the stable. Denise asked Mrs. Garcia if they could go. She said, "It is too hard for me to walk. You go. I stay here at the *nacimiento*."

Espie and Denise made their way slowly through the crowd. The street lights came on and their glow shadowed the animals until they looked real to Espie. There's nothing like this in the barrio, she thought. Then she remembered the Plaza she stood in, the church across the way, and Olvera Street itself were the foundations of the mess that was Los Angeles. The area had been settled by families from Mexico. She said to Denise, "How did we lose all this to you paddies?"

"It's still yours," Denise said.

But it wasn't. It was a tourist attraction. Something the city said was worth saving.

Espie made her way back toward the stable. "I wonder if they'll save our barrio," she said.

They eased their way through the crowd to the shops. "When does *las posadas* start?" Espie asked Mrs. Garcia.

"Soon. They begin at the Avila Adobe."

Espie stood on the steps that led to one of the shops so

she could see what was happening. "There're people dressed like Mary and Joseph over there."

Mrs. Garcia said, "Then we must go so we can have candles."

She started toward the adobe, and Espie asked Denise, "What does she mean?"

"We're going to take part in the procession," Denise told her.

"How?"

"We carry candles behind Mary and Joseph and sing with them when they ask for a place to stay at the shops."

The narrow street was a body of people, and when Espie reached the adobe, somebody handed her a candle. "What do we do now?" she asked.

Mrs. Garcia said, "We wait."

The mariachi band had stopped playing, and voices and laughter filled the street. Denise said, "There's Teresa."

Mrs. Garcia looked in the direction Denise pointed. "That is Raul with her?" she asked Espie.

Espie stretched to see over people's heads. Teresa waved. Espie said, "Yeah, that's Raul."

Mrs. Garcia said, "They come see us."

Teresa introduced Raul to Mrs. Garcia and Denise. Mrs. Garcia told Raul, "The ladies at church tell me the nice things you do." He smiled and thanked her.

Teresa pulled Espie aside while Mrs. Garcia talked to Raul. "I'm sorry about last night," she said. "You still coming to TJ?"

"Not with that nut."

"You have to. I don't want to go alone with him."

"Then don't," Espie said.

Teresa's frightened eyes made it obvious Raul would make her go. "Okay," Espie said. "I'll go, but only . . ." Espie looked away.

"Only what?"

"Nothing," Espie said. She couldn't say, "But only because I'm afraid for you."

Raul said to Teresa, "They're forming the procession. Let's move over there." He pointed past the adobe.

Mrs. Garcia asked, "You not walk with Mary and Joseph?"

Raul said, "Not this time."

Somebody lit Espie's candle, and Denise and Mrs. Garcia lit theirs from the flame. Mrs. Garcia said, "He is a nice boy."

People lined up in front of them and behind them. They waited to move. Espie saw Teresa and Raul on the steps of a shop next to the adobe. A man walked toward them and said something to Raul. He moved away. The procession started and people sang, *"En el nombre de cielo . . ."* "In the name of heaven . . ." The man touched Raul's arm. Anger masked his face. As Espie passed, Raul broke away. He shouted to Teresa, "Let's go."

The man called, "Señor, señor."

Raul grabbed Teresa's hand and pushed people out of his way. She tripped and almost fell to the ground. He pulled her and disappeared in the crowd.

Chapter 10

When the procession ended, the children took turns trying to break the piñata shaped like a Santa Claus that hung in the center of the street. They scrambled for the candies that scattered on the ground after the paper-covered, plaster Santa Claus broke. Espie laughed at the children's shouts and giggles as they picked up handfuls of candy. The last time she had helped break a piñata had been on her eleventh birthday. So many things had stopped after her father left.

Mrs. Garcia said, "We must go. It is getting late. And Espie, you are cold with only the sweater."

"It's not bad," Espie lied. "The crowd helped to keep me warm."

But she was frozen. She couldn't even get warm on the bus because although the driver had a small heater, the rest of the bus didn't. Her teeth chattered while she walked home in the dark. She hoped Mrs. Garcia would turn on the wall heater, but she didn't. She never turned it on at night. "It is too expensive," she always said.

Espie undressed quickly and got under the covers. She pulled her knees up to her chest and rolled into a ball under the thin blankets. She was still cold, but the trip had been worth it. The procession was beautiful. And a couple of times during the ceremony she found herself praying—for her father wherever he was, for her grandmother. And for Teresa. Espie remembered Raul's anger at the man who approached him. Why should Raul be so mad? Or was he scared?

Surely he couldn't be afraid of such a small man. He didn't look like he even weighed a hundred and fifty pounds, and his head barely reached Raul's shoulder.

Espie pulled her body into a tighter ball. She wondered what she would do if she were Teresa. Espie decided she'd run away, but she had done that and it hadn't solved anything. Besides, Teresa wasn't the type of person who would run away. Espie wished she could help her, but she had promised not to fink. Even if she did, Mary Parks hadn't given Espie much hope. Espie pulled the blankets over her head. After we get back from TJ, I'll do something, she thought. But what? She fell asleep before she could think of anything.

Monday night she worked the desk and Wednesday she sold Christmas trees. She wished they had one in the house, but she'd have to be satisfied with the stable. Presents from girls Mrs. Garcia had helped surrounded it, and Denise had wrapped the votive candle and put it with the other gifts. Espie hated to give the present of time Denise had suggested, but it looked like she'd have to. Christmas was less than a week away and she still didn't have anything for Mrs. Garcia.

The tree lot was very empty. The only trees left were the scrawny ones and the expensive ones, but people kept buying. Espie wondered if Parks had meant what she said about saving part of the sale profits for a trip to Europe.

Thursday morning Teresa phoned. She said, "We'll pick you up at ten, okay?"

Espie said, "Okay, I'll be ready."

"Good. Raul doesn't like to wait."

Espie's fingers tightened on the phone. "Tell Raul to . . ." she relaxed. "Never mind. I'll be ready at ten," she said, and hung up. When they got back from Tijuana she'd tell him to go to hell herself.

When the truck pulled up at five minutes to ten, Espie walked to it slowly. "Hi," she said through the open window, and turned the door handle. Teresa moved closer to Raul to make room for Espie, and he put the truck into gear without even saying hello.

But halfway down the block, he said, "It's great of you to help. Some of the presents were already wrapped when I got them, but we still have a lot to do. I don't know if we could get them all finished without your help."

It was the first time he'd said anything nice to her. Espie was so surprised, all she could say was, "Yeah, well, I'm glad to help."

Raul stopped in front of a small duplex. The grass and bushes were neatly trimmed. The white paint was unmarked by the spray paint grafitti that covered so many walls in the barrio. Espie asked, "How does the owner keep it so clean?"

"I'm the owner and the kids know I'll bash their faces in if they mess with my property." He got out of the truck and walked around to the sidewalk. "I just had it painted," he said, and smiled. And Espie smiled back, happy that even the great Raul of the barrio didn't escape the gangs.

He unlocked the door and stood aside for the girls to go in. The apartment looked like Raul's clothes. Everything matched, everything fit just right. Even the Christmas presents that stood in the corner of the room looked as though they belonged just where they were.

Raul closed the door and hung his keys on the hook by the door. "How do you like the place?" he asked.

Espie said, "It's nice, really nice." She saw bottled plants like the ones she had seen at Teresa's house. And, just like the ones at Teresa's, they all had tops on them. "You have plants like Teresa's," Espie said. She walked to one and examined the bottle.

Raul said, "Wrong. Teresa has plants like mine. I taught her how to fix them."

"How do you get plants inside the bottles like that?" Espie asked.

"If the top of the bottle is wide enough, it's not too hard to get the dirt and the plant in. But when you get a bottle with a tiny neck, the plant is hard to fix."

"Do you take the cover off to water it?"

"After it's planted in there, I never take off the cover."

Espie looked at the plant closer. "How does it stay alive all sealed up like that?"

Teresa said, "You make sure there's enough moisture and air before you seal it up, then the plant makes its own. It'll live for years."

"How?" Espie asked.

Raul smiled, a smile that told Espie how stupid he thought she was. But Espie was too curious to care what he thought. He said, "It's like this. During the day, plants breathe in carbon dioxide and . . ."

Espie interrupted, "What's carbon dioxide?"

Raul gave her that same smile again. "It's what people breathe out. Look, don't interrupt me and I think I can explain it so even you'll understand. See, people breathe in oxygen and breathe out carbon dioxide. They do this night and day. But during the day, plants breathe in carbon dioxide, then breathe out oxygen during the night."

Espie said, "But . . ."

Raul held up his hand to stop her. "Then at night they breathe in oxygen and breathe out carbon dioxide. That way they always have what they need to live."

Espie asked, "What about water?"

"The water I put in evaporates inside the container and can't get out because the bottle is plugged up. The moisture from that water makes it 'rain' on the plant."

"Think I could fix a plant like that?" Espie asked.

Raul said, "Anybody can if they know how."

"How long would it take me? I mean, could I do it in the next couple of days?"

Teresa asked, "Why the next couple of days?"

"I want to give one to Mrs. Garcia for Christmas."

Raul said, "Tell you what. I've got a real nice wine bottle I've been saving for a terrarium—that's what these things are called, you know. I'll give it to you. I'll even help you fix it up. Okay?"

Espie searched his face to see if he was making fun of her. "You mean it?"

He shrugged, "Sure. You help me. I help you."

Espie laughed. "It's a deal," she said, relieved that she'd have something near the stable along with the presents from other girls Mrs. Garcia had helped.

Raul said, "Okay, let's get busy on these packages."

Espie liked to wrap presents. She hadn't wrapped many in her life, so it was fun to put red, green, or silver paper on the toys and clothes. Most of them didn't have boxes and that made the job harder to do, but she managed with a lot of Scotch tape.

Raul seemed to wrap two presents for every one she finished, and each one he did was beautiful. Raul liked beautiful things and, if what was in the package wasn't always beautiful, his wrappings were.

Espie was disappointed at most of the gifts. She had thought people had given pretty dresses and shoes because they wanted the families in Tijuana to have nice clothes. But although Espie didn't know much about style, she knew that much of what had been given to Raul were things factory owners or store managers would have trouble selling.

After she picked up one dress that was even uglier than the others she had wrapped, she said, "Nobody's going to wear this thing."

Teresa said, "The people Raul helps wear everything he gives them because they have nothing else. I told you, Espie, you don't know what poor is until you've seen these people."

Espie knew what poor was. It was not being able to buy a coke on a hot day on the way home from school. It was making believe it didn't matter not being able to go to the movie everybody said was great. It was freezing in a sweater while other people wrapped up in shawls and coats. "I'm not exactly having problems with my extra million bucks," she said. Teresa laughed and Espie picked up a T-shirt with the words L.A. MUSEC CENTER printed on it—the word *music* was spelled with an *e* instead of an *i*. "If people are going to give things, why don't they give nice things?"

Raul shrugged. "These are the things people can't sell. They give them to me and call it charity. That way they can take a lot of money off their income tax."

So that was it. People didn't give to help others. They gave to help themselves. But what about Raul? Espie watched him put a red ribbon on a silver package. What was he getting out of it? He put the package on top of the presents that were already wrapped. She couldn't believe he was doing this to help people. He must be getting something out of it. I'm beginning to think like a pig, she thought, and chuckled.

Raul asked, "What's so funny?"

"Nothing," Espie said, and reached for another present.

At twelve thirty Raul said, "Keep wrapping and I'll fix some sandwiches." He went into the kitchen and Espie heard him humming while he worked.

Within minutes he called them in to eat. He'd made ham sandwiches and put a gallon of chocolate milk on the table. Espie filled her glass the moment she sat down. She'd had chocolate milk only twice in her life and she loved it.

Raul talked about their trip and his woodworking while they ate. He didn't seem to notice Espie and Teresa didn't say anything. He didn't even pay attention when Espie filled her glass again with chocolate milk.

When they finished eating, he was still talking about woodworking. He stood up. "Come in here," he said to Espie.

She and Teresa followed him to the living room. He pointed to the table in front of the couch. "What do you think that is?" he asked.

Espie looked at the highly polished, beautifully decorated piece of furniture. "It's a coffee table," she said.

Raul chuckled. "What else is it?"

Espie walked closer to the table. She shrugged. She hated stupid questions. "I give up," she said.

Raul said, "It's a game board. You open it up and you can play more than a dozen games." He pointed to the table. "Go ahead. Open it."

Teresa's expression told Espie she didn't have any

chance of opening it. Espie tried to pull the top off. She pushed it. She pulled it. It didn't move and she couldn't see any place where the table would open.

Espie sat on the couch. "Okay, show me," she said.

Raul laughed. "There's a secret button in one of the carved roses. "See?" He pressed the center of a flower. The table didn't open.

Espie said, "Looks like you're stuck with a coffee table."

Raul's eyes laughed at her. He pressed another button at the same time as he pressed the first button he had pushed, and the table top moved. His expression told Espie he knew he was a genius.

Espie looked for Teresa. She had gone back to wrapping presents. Espie went to help her and Raul closed his game table. She asked, "What good is it? I mean, it's pretty, but why didn't you just make a coffee table and a game table instead of carving all that fancy woodwork to hide the opening and buttons?"

"I like to own things other people can't have." He looked at Teresa, and Espie wondered if Teresa realized that to Raul she was just a coffee table.

There were a dozen trucks to wrap. And there was something wrong with each one of them, but Espie knew the kids who got them wouldn't care.

"Where did you get the paper to wrap all these things?" she asked.

"A guy downtown gave it to me." Espie looked at the paper closer to see what was wrong with it. Raul laughed. "It's okay. This guy's really hung up on charity. He gives only good stuff." He picked up a pair of sandals and began to wrap them. "There's a lot of nice things in the packages that were already wrapped. People in the barrio are very generous."

They worked mostly in silence, and at three thirty Espie was glad to hear Raul say he was quitting for the day. "We can finish these tomorrow and still have time to load up the truck. Come on outside. I'll fix Mrs. Garcia's terrarium."

"Now?"

"Sure, the bottle and stuff are in the garage."

Teresa said, "I'll keep wrapping until you've finished the terrarium."

"I want you with me," Raul said, smiling, but his lips were tight against his teeth and his eyes were hard.

Teresa clutched the pointed scissors she had used to cut paper. Her hand grew white from the tightness. Espie took a step toward her. Teresa dropped the scissors and walked toward the back door.

They went into the small garage behind the house. Raul took a bottle from one of the shelves and held it toward Espie. It was shaped like a violin and had a pink glow to it. "It's beautiful," she said.

"I told you it was. I was going to keep it for myself, but this Mrs. Garcia is pretty special, isn't she?" Espie nodded. "Okay. Let's get what you want to plant."

The grass was green and well kept. Poinsettias bloomed at one end of the yard. Their red leaves drew Espie to them.

"Those won't work," Raul said. "You have to have strong plants. Cactus is the best." He strolled toward the other end of the yard to a cactus garden. "Pick any kind you want," he said.

Espie had never paid much attention to cactus. It was something that grew everywhere, but Raul had plants she had never seen. "Can I take more than one kind?"

"Sure, pick three and I can fix them up real nice."

"How you going to do that through that small bottle opening?" Espie asked.

"We use the smallest plants. Besides, I've worked with openings smaller than that."

"How?"

"Pick your plants and I'll show you." His voice grew impatient.

Espie pointed to two kinds of cactus she had never seen and to one she had always liked because the cactus itself was shaped like a flower.

Raul dug up the tiny plants at the bottom of the larger ones and carried them back to the garage. Espie walked beside him and Teresa followed them. She hadn't said a word since they left the house. She reminded Espie of an obedient puppy.

Raul got a funnel and poured stuff in the bottle. Espie asked, "What's that?"

"Special soil and charcoal. They keep the plants healthy." He took a long piece of steel, picked up one of the plants with it and placed it in the bottle.

"They work like fingers," Espie said.

Raul picked up another cactus and put it in the bottle. After the three plants were inside he used narrow sticks to fix the plants. He moved them over and over. Each time, he put down the bottle in the sun, stepped back, and looked at it. He did this again and again until finally he smiled and asked, "What do you think?"

Espie said, "It's beautiful."

Raul looked at Teresa. "It's beautiful," she repeated.

Raul said, "I love beautiful things." And the way he looked at Teresa, Espie knew that he would never let her go. She was the most beautiful thing he owned.

Chapter 11

Raul said he'd wrap Mrs. Garcia's present so Espie wouldn't disturb the plants, and she was glad to let him. He chose silver paper and a red ribbon and topped it off with a large bow. When he finished, Espie thought it was the prettiest package she'd ever seen.

"I hope I can sneak it in the house without Mrs. Garcia seeing it."

Teresa asked, "Don't you want her to know you're giving her a present?"

"Well, you know, she doesn't have any money to get me anything, and I don't want her to think she has to go out and buy something because I'm giving her a present." She held the package away from her so she wouldn't wrinkle the paper or mess up the bow. "Thanks a lot, Raul," she said.

He took his keys from the hook by the front door. "That's okay. I told you. You help me and I help you. That's the way people should be." He opened the door, and, for a moment, Espie decided Raul wasn't getting anything out of his trips to Mexico except the fun of helping people.

During the ride home, Espie held the present on her lap with the bow carefully on top. "What time are we leaving Saturday?" she asked.

Raul said, "Around nine thirty."

Espie asked, "How long does it take to get there?"

Teresa said, "Two and a half to three hours."

Espie asked her, "You ever been there?"

"I've been to different places in Mexico with my parents, but this is the first time with Raul."

Raul smiled. "Maybe you'll come with me all the time now. What do you think?" He stopped the truck in front of Mrs. Garcia's and Espie got out before Teresa had a chance to answer.

Raul called, "We'll pick you up at ten again tomorrow."

Espie waved and hurried up the walk. She climbed the stairs and listened at the door. The old sewing machine was running. She decided to try to put the package on the stuffed chair that faced the television before Mrs. Garcia looked up. Espie opened the door, slipped the present on the chair, and started toward the kitchen.

Mrs. Garcia asked, "Did you have a nice time?"

"We did a lot of work, but it was fun."

Mrs. Garcia turned back to the sewing machine. "We will have soup soon. I must finish this skirt now so I can sew the hem tonight." She sighed. "Everybody want their clothes for Christmas."

Espie went back to the chair for the present and hurried to her room. When Denise saw her she asked, "What Santa Claus did you rip off?"

"It's a terrarium. You know, a garden in a bottle."

Denise nodded. "I know. Some kids made them last year in my science class."

"At Franklin Heights?"

Denise laughed. "You're going to have to pay more attention to what's going on at that school." She watched Espie put the package under her bed. "Did you make it yourself?"

"No, Raul fixed it. It's beautiful. The bottle is shaped like a violin and the glass is just a little bit pink. When the sun shines on it, it glows."

Denise pulled her legs under her and sat Indian-style on her bed. "Does Teresa really like that guy? I mean, he's kind of old for her, isn't he?"

"Yeah, I guess he is," Espie said, and ignored the first question. She took her uniform blouse from the closet. "I have to iron this thing for inspection tonight."

"Skip it. Officer Parks called. She said she didn't want the L.E.E.G.s to wear their uniforms."

Espie put the blouse back. "Why not?"

"I don't know. She said we can wear anything we want. She'd rather we didn't wear jeans, but she said it was okay if we did."

"It has to be jeans. What else have I got?"

Denise stood up and walked to the closet. "I don't know whether to wear my brown dress or the purple one."

Espie watched Denise take the purple dress out, then put it back and take out the brown one. At least Espie didn't have to make decisions.

The L.E.E.G. meeting began with the pledge of allegiance like all the others, the roll call, and finally the arguments about which girls had paid their dues and which ones hadn't. But when that was done, Parks took over the meeting instead of Alice Eliott.

The officer said, "There're small paper pads and pencils in front of each of you. I want you to take them and go stand, face toward the wall."

Questions and movement filled the room. Mary Parks said, "I won't answer questions, just do what I told you."

Espie picked up the pad and pencil and strolled to the end of the room. Officer Parks said, "Come on, everybody face the wall." The girls murmured and turned around. " 'Tention," the woman said, and immediately the room grew quiet.

"Okay, now listen up. This is a training session to see how observant you are. I asked you not to wear uniforms because I want each girl to describe what another girl is wearing—don't move. You've been together about twenty minutes, longer for those who came early. Alice, I want you to write on your pad what Roxanne is wearing. Roxanne, I want you to describe what Denise is wearing. Denise, you write what Jean is wearing." Mary Parks named each girl. Espie got a new girl named Connie.

She was a recruit and Espie wasn't even sure what the girl looked like. Mary Parks said, "At ease. And I want a full description—color, style, shoes, special decorations, anything that will make that person stand out."

Espie guessed jeans, a green sweater, and black shoes. With any luck she'd hit one out of three. She told Mary Parks, "I'm finished. Can I turn around now?"

"No, I have something else to ask you." Espie stood on one foot, then the other. Finally, the officer said, "You've been holding meetings in this office for months. I want you to write down what's on the captain's desk. During the day it's cluttered with paperwork, but he's a neat man. When he leaves, his desk always looks the same and that's the way you see it. I want you to write down everything you can think of that's on his desk."

Complaints came from each side of Espie. Parks said, "You have two minutes."

Espie wrote, "A gold frame with pictures of three children." She'd looked at those smiling faces often enough. "A black pen-and-pencil set, a telephone, a wooden holder for papers, an ashtray, a cigarette lighter, a large eraser with the words I NEVER MAKE BIG MISTAKES printed on it." She closed her eyes and tried to think of something else. "A letter opener, a clock, a trophy." Was there anything else? She couldn't think of anything, so for good measure she wrote, "On the wall behind the desk is a sign that SAYS, WE CAN TOLERATE STUPID QUESTIONS, BUT WE CAN'T TOLERATE STUPID PEOPLE."

Parks said, "Okay, everybody sit down and let's see how you did."

Espie turned toward the girl named Connie. She was wearing a brown skirt, a gold blouse, and brown shoes. Espie had been wrong all the way. She looked at the desk and saw she'd done better there.

Mary Parks said, "Look at the girl you were asked to describe. How many of you did it a hundred percent?" Not one hand went up. "Who got the colors right?" A few girls raised their hands. Parks asked questions until she got to "How many didn't get anything right?" Espie and Roxanne raised their hands. Everybody laughed.

Espie snapped, "Wait until we get to the desk part."

Parks asked, "How did you do, Espie?"

"I got everything."

The officer asked, "How many of you did that?"

Nobody moved. Espie put her thumbs in the belt loops of her jeans and looked around the table. "Just think how great I'd be describing a murder room."

Alice said, "Terrific, but I hope you never have to describe the murderer."

Mary Parks smiled. "Okay, let's try something else."

Connie raised her hand. "Why are we doing this?"

Officer Parks said, "Two of the best crime-prevention weapons a policeman has are his eyes. An officer patrols his beat with his eyes always ready to catch something that's not right, not normal. Maybe it's a light in a store that should be on, but isn't. Maybe it's a light that shouldn't be on, but is. He's always searching. I want you to get in the habit of seeing and hearing what's around you. It's a good habit, even if you never intend to become a police officer. For instance, you might become a nurse." Parks glanced at Espie.

"Sometimes people trained in medicine can tell something's wrong with a person before that person even knows it himself. And you can learn a lot about people by the way they dress or walk or talk. That comes in handy in almost anything you do." She took a stack of papers from a table behind her. "I'm going to pass these out face down. Don't turn them over until I tell you." When she finished, she said, "Now, I'm going to show you a picture, and let you look at it for ten seconds before I take it away. On the other side of those papers are questions about the picture, so look at it hard. The more you see, the more questions you'll be able to answer."

She put up a picture of a crowded street corner. There were people and cars. Children played in the background. Almost immediately the picture was gone. The girls complained they didn't have enough time to examine it.

Mary Parks said, "An officer sometimes only has a couple of seconds to take in a scene. You had ten. Now turn over your papers and answer whatever questions you can."

Espie looked at her paper. The first question was, "What was the color of the hair of the man who was leaning against the green car?" The second question was, "In what direction was he looking?"

The girls' moans told Espie she wasn't the only one who didn't know the answers. Out of ten questions, she only answered one. And when Mary Parks told them time was up and gave them the answers, Espie was relieved to know the most questions anybody answered were four and some girls didn't get any.

The police officer said, "It isn't as easy as it sounds, is it? Okay, let's do it with another picture." She passed out more papers. Before the meeting broke up she did it nine more times, and each time everybody's score improved. On the last test Espie got eight out of ten correct and a couple of the girls got them all right. "The L.A. criminal is finished," Espie said. "He'll never get away with anything now."

Mary Parks said, "He will if he's not a desk," and Espie laughed.

Espie and Denise told Carlos about the training session on the way home. Carlos said, "Here's something else to remember. When there's a crowd of people, watch the person who's not doing what the others are doing. Like one night, I was patrolling at a bazaar and a lot of people were around the dunking booth. You know, the one where people pay a quarter to try to hit a board that knocks somebody in a tank of water? Well, people were laughing and yelling for the pitcher to aim better, but there was one guy who was just looking, and every so often moved to another place. He was picking pockets. I got an officer and we arrested him with the evidence still on him."

When they stopped in front of Mrs. Garcia's, he said, "If either of you wants to work the desk Monday afternoon, I'll give you a ride to the station."

Denise asked, "What duty did you volunteer for this time?"

"None. I'm going on patrol with Gary Horton and Ron Peters in the ride-along program."

Espie asked, "How did you work that?"

"My captain recommended me for it. He said I put in more volunteer hours than anybody in the Post."

Denise said, "That's great, Carlos."

Espie opened the door. "I'll call Officer Parks and tell her I'll go down. Maybe if I volunteer for enough stuff, I can get in on this ride-along thing."

Denise said, "It takes a lot of hours."

Espie shrugged. "I've got a lot of hours."

Chapter 12

It was hot Friday morning when Raul and Teresa picked up Espie. She seldom tied her hair back. She liked the way she looked with it hanging loose. But this morning, she wore a rubber band to hold it because she knew the hair would get in her way while she worked. Despite the heat, Teresa still wore her wig. Espie hadn't seen Teresa without the wig since the day after Gary Horton and Ron Peters had brought her to the police station.

Espie looked at the miniature house on the back of the truck as she hopped into the pickup. She asked Raul, "Did you make the house?" He nodded.

"Built it myself in a couple of weeks. Except for the carvings on the inside walls. Those took me months to do." He stopped behind a line of traffic. "Most people just go out and buy a plastic camper thing to put on their trucks, but I like things other people can't have." He glanced at Teresa before he shifted gears and moved again.

Espie wondered if Teresa felt owned. She looked tired. Had she looked tired at other times, and Espie hadn't noticed because she never paid that much attention to people? She wanted to tell Teresa about the identification experiments Mary Parks had done during the L.E.E.G. meeting but decided against it, so they rode in silence until Teresa asked, "Did you get the present in the house without Mrs. Garcia seeing it?"

Espie nodded. "I put it under my bed."

Teresa asked, "Won't she find it?"

"Denise and I clean the room. Mrs. Garcia never does it."

Raul said, "Why should you clean her house?"

"Because it's my home," Espie told him, and realized it was the first time she had thought of it that way. Until then, it had always been Mrs. Garcia's house.

Raul stopped in front of his duplex. It was still unmarked by the spray paint grafitti. But the gangs were usually quiet on Thursday night. Espie was willing to bet they'd hit the house over the weekend. It was cool inside and Raul closed the door behind them to keep it that way.

They went right to work, and after they finished wrapping the clothes, they began to wrap dolls. Espie touched their hair and smoothed their clothes. Raul said, "If you're going to play all day we'll never finish." He put a ribbon on the package he had just wrapped. "Put the letter *g* on the packages with the dolls," he said.

Espie asked, "Why?"

Raul said, "So we won't give a doll to a boy."

"What's wrong with that?" Espie asked.

Teresa said, "What would a boy do with a doll?"

Espie said, "Play with it."

Raul laughed until he realized she was serious, and his eyes grew angry. "Mexican boys don't play with dolls."

Espie said, "Why not? They're going to be fathers, aren't they?"

Raul snapped, "Mexican men don't take care of babies. That's a woman's job," and Teresa looked as though she agreed with him. Espie shrugged and put a *b* on the package while Raul wasn't looking. It was time boys learned how to take care of babies, even Mexican boys.

They took a lunch break and finished working around three. Raul picked up one of the boxes filled with presents. "We better get them on the truck," he said, and headed for the back door.

Teresa and Espie picked up boxes and followed him. He hopped inside, put down his box, and took the one Espie was carrying. She stretched to see inside. "Come on in. You may as well see it before we get it loaded up."

Espie went up the two steps and Teresa followed her. A green shag rug covered the floor and the same kind of carved wooden roses that were on the coffee table decorated the sides of the door and windows. There was a long seat covered with red cushions below each window. Espie said, "I guess if you press the right roses, one of the seats turns into a table and the other one turns into a television."

Raul laughed. "No, the seats are just to sit on and for storage." He picked up the lid on one of them. "See, no hidden openings."

Teresa said, "If you're going to stand around all day and talk, we'll never get finished." Her voice was sharp.

Raul glared at her, then shrugged. "Yeah, we'd better get it done. We won't have time in the morning."

Espie made trip after trip with Raul and Teresa. Neither of them said a word. Espie thought, They act like they've been married for years and they hate each other for it.

On the way home, Espie pulled off the rubber band from her hair and let it fall free. Teresa watched her run her fingers through it to comb it out. Espie suddenly felt uncomfortable. Before she got home, she decided not to see Teresa and Raul after they got back from Tijuana. Espie could ignore Raul's insults, but she couldn't ignore Teresa's silence and her moods.

Gary Horton and Ron Peters had been right when they told Espie not to get involved with people she met on the job. And Denise had warned Espie that she wouldn't be able to live a life of her own if she became too involved.

That's what had happened, and Espie didn't like it. She had earned the trip to Tijuana with her two days of work, so she'd take it. But when they came back, she'd cut out. That's the way she felt when she got out of the truck and said, "See you in the morning." But by the time she went to bed, she had changed her mind. You didn't leave a friend in trouble any more than you finked on one.

While Espie ate breakfast, Mrs. Garcia fixed peanut butter and jelly sandwiches. "You will be hungry on the way and I cannot give you money."

Espie took a bite of her toast. "That's okay," she said. She hoped Teresa and Raul would bring sandwiches so they wouldn't lose time stopping at McDonald's or Jack-in-the-Box. She was anxious to get to Tijuana. Besides, she'd hate to watch them eat hamburgers while she ate peanut butter and jelly.

Espie hadn't even finished saying hello to Teresa before Raul stepped on the gas and lurched the truck down the middle of the street.

"Hey, take it easy," Espie said.

"Shut up," Raul told her.

Espie said, "Look, if this is how you're going to be, let me off. I'm not going to TJ with a fruitcake."

Raul said, "Those bastards spray painted the walls of the duplex last night."

Espie pictured the spotless walls sprayed with black letters and stifled a laugh. "Why don't you paint a mural?

The barrio is full of them and the gangs don't touch them."

Raul turned onto Broadway with tires screeching, and Espie decided if she was going to live through the trip to Tijuana, she'd better keep her ideas to herself. But she liked the brilliant murals of barrio life, Aztec warriors and Mexican heroes painted on walls and fences. Some areas looked like giant art galleries, and paddies were beginning to come see the primitive art painted by professional artists, school children, and anybody else who felt like beautifying the area. Even members of the violent Arizona Gang had helped do the Virgin of Guadalupe mural which was one of Espie's favorites. She wondered what a suitable mural would be for Raul's duplex and decided an old bridegroom hobbling down the church steps with a young bride who danced around him while she threw flowers at young dudes.

Raul slowed down for the freeway entrance and weaved through the heavy traffic to the Santa Ana Freeway. That was the one she had taken to go to Disneyland. "We going to pass Disneyland?" she asked.

Teresa said, "We'll even see the top of the Matterhorn."

Espie asked, "You ever been on it?" She had taken the ride with Carlos the day after she graduated from the police academy.

"A few times, but the lines are always so long, Raul never wants to wait."

That figures, Espie thought.

Raul snapped on the radio and music blared through the truck, making conversation difficult, if not impossible. Espie took the hint and shut up. She read the forest of billboards that advertised everything from suntan lotion to homes for *only* $75,000. Raul weaved in and out of traffic. A marker said, SAN DIEGO—99 MILES. Espie clutched her bag with the peanut butter and jelly sandwiches. It was going to be a long trip.

She watched the mileage signs to Disneyland and spotted the top of the Matterhorn. "There it is," she said.

Teresa asked, "You come to Disneyland a lot?"

"Only once. The Explorers paid for everything. We had a wild time."

Raul raised the radio volume and switched the dial. Immediately the music changed from the latest U.S. hits to Mexican music. His actions told her to shut up, but she didn't care. She liked the music, and when the announcer said in Spanish, "This is Radio 95, Tijuana," Espie stared out the window and looked for signs that gave the mileage to Tijuana. There weren't any. But there was one that said, SAN DIEGO—89 MILES, then 79, then 69. Finally she asked, "How far is Tijuana from San Diego?"

Raul said, "Sixteen miles." And Espie added sixteen to every sign she saw about San Diego.

There were fewer billboards. Green hills rose and fell as far as she could see and suddenly there was water. "There's the ocean!" Espie yelled.

Raul said, "Yeah, it's been there a million years."

"Well, I never saw it before."

Teresa said, "How can you live in California and not see the ocean?"

"East Los Angeles isn't exactly Santa Monica Beach, you know."

Raul spotted a Jack-in-the-Box. He slowed down for the off-ramp. "Better pick up the hamburgers here, then we can eat while we drive." He circled the concrete ribbon that brought him within a block of the drive-in.

Teresa asked Espie, "What are you going to have?"

Espie opened her lunch bag. "I've got a couple of sandwiches."

Raul drove up to the box and said, "Two hamburgers and two chocolate shakes." A voice repeated the order and Raul drove up to the pick-up window. He paid the girl for the food and handed the bag to Teresa so he could maneuver his way back on the freeway.

The odor from the hamburgers filled the truck. Espie took a bite of her peanut butter and jelly sandwich and felt the way she did when she watched kids gulp cokes on hot days at school.

As soon as they got back on the freeway, Teresa opened the bag and unwrapped one of the hamburgers. She handed it to Raul, then pulled out a milk shake. Some of it had spilled over the top and dripped down the side. A drop fell on Raul's pants. He moved his leg and the car jerked. "You clumsy bitch."

"Don't yell at me," Teresa said.

Espie almost choked on her sandwich. She stared at Teresa, whose face changed immediately from anger to fear. Espie gave her arm a squeeze that said, "That's telling him off," but Teresa didn't look at her. She was too busy trying to clean off the spot with spit on a Kleenex.

Raul pushed her away. "Leave it alone. You'll make it worse."

Teresa wiped the paper cup with the Kleenex, put the straw through the hole in the top of the cup, and said, "I'm sorry."

"That won't help when I show up in front of those people in dirty clothes."

Espie could hardly see the spot. He was a nut, a real nut. She knew a lot of them, but if anybody took a vote, Raul would be king of them all.

He steered with the hamburger in one hand and the milk shake in the other. Espie was happy when he shoved the last piece of burger in his mouth and happier still when she heard the slurp that told her he had reached the bottom of the cup.

Teresa put the cup in the bag and Espie crumbled her brown paper bag in a ball and put it in. Teresa said, "Want some of my shake?"

Peanut butter still clung to the top of Espie's mouth. "Yeah, thanks," she said, and took a couple of long draws on the straw before she gave it back. She was thirsty, but she would rather live all her life without a milk shake than be Raul's girl for five minutes.

She saw a sign that said INTERNATIONAL BORDER, 2 MILES, and in a moment the cars slowed to a crawl.

"What's happening?" Espie asked.

Teresa said, "We have to get past the gates."

Markers on the ground kept the cars from cutting in and out of lines as they edged toward a booth. Raul turned off the radio. A man in a brown uniform glanced in the truck and waved them on.

"We in Mexico?" Espie asked.

Teresa said, "Almost."

They crawled to another booth and approached a man in a dark green uniform that said MEXICO on the sleeve. He waved them on, the way the other man had done.

Immediately they were surrounded by people, noise, and cars that all seemed to be going in different directions. Kids jumped dangerously close to the truck, "Serapes? Lamps? Purses?" they yelled. Espie shook her head. "A wallet?" Espie told them no. "Five dollars," the boy closest to the truck said. Espie shook her head again. "Three fifty," the boy said.

Teresa told her, "He'll come down to two."

Espie told the boy, "I don't have any money."

He shrugged and ran to join the other kids, who were already attacking the cars behind the pickup.

Raul made a right turn, then a left turn, and crossed a bridge. "Beggars," he muttered.

"This is Mexico?" Espie said. She couldn't believe what she saw was the Mexico she had wanted to see so much.

Teresa said, "It's TJ. You have to drive farther in to see the real Mexico. It's beautiful."

Raul almost hit a car that made a turn without signaling. He swore at the driver. A man carried two live chickens past stalks of bananas hung from hooks beside leather jackets and silver jewelry. Women, their arms filled with giant paper flowers, tried to force them on tourists; a boy did the same with plaster statues he displayed in the trunk of his car. A man held up a tray of churros. Espie loved the long sweet doughnuts, but she couldn't buy one.

Raul made several turns. The crowds thinned. Fewer cars were on the streets. And soon they went from concrete to a dirt road. Dust flew all around them. Espie choked and closed the window she had opened at the border. "Where we going?"

"I promised the people on the hill I'd come to their village this trip," Raul said. His words were quiet and directed at her as though he had been a perfect gentleman during the whole trip.

Espie thought, He's getting ready to do his thing. And whatever it was, it included having her and Teresa with him.

Before they were halfway up the hill, children started to run toward the truck. Their shouts brought out their parents, and in a moment the crowd surrounded the truck so Raul had to stop. People shouted "Feliz Navidad" and clung to the pickup.

Raul laughed. "Move away so I can go farther down the road," he said in Spanish, but people paid no attention to him. Finally he shrugged, turned off the ignition, and got out of the truck. A woman clasped his hand. "God bless you," she said. Children clung to his legs. Men slapped him on the back. Espie wondered if this was why he made the trips to Mexico. Everybody wants to be loved, and at this moment Raul seemed to be loved.

But Teresa asked, "Do you think they really love him?" as though she had read Espie's thoughts and didn't believe anybody could love Raul.

Espie said, "They act like they do."

"Maybe they just want his presents." The jabbering beside the truck almost drowned out her words.

Espie said, "When we get back to Los Angeles tell him to go find an old chick."

"I can't."

"Why not?"

"I'm afraid of what he'll do to me," she whispered.

Raul reached into the truck and clasped Teresa's hand. "Come meet my friends," he said. Teresa pulled her hand away. Raul's smile didn't fade, but his eyes ordered her out. She slid under the steering wheel and stood beside him. Espie followed her, certain Teresa was right. Raul could be dangerous and Espie didn't know how to protect her.

A small boy pulled Raul's sleeve. "Can we have presents now?" he asked in Spanish.

Raul laughed. "Why not?" He picked up the boy and put him on his shoulders. He started for the back of the truck and people moved away to clear a path. The boy's feet were bare and dusty, but Raul ignored the dirt the child left on his spotless embroidered shirt. Children pressed close to him and put their filthy hands on his pants, but the smile didn't leave his face. He was their hero and he loved it. Teresa could have spilled the whole milk shake on his pants and these people wouldn't have noticed. Espie wondered if he yelled at Teresa just to keep her scared.

When he reached the door of the small house on the back of the pickup, he swung the boy to the ground, put the key in the lock, and opened the door. Everybody rushed to look inside. Espie fell against the truck. "Hey, watch it," she said to the boy closest to her.

She spoke in English, but the boy answered in Spanish, "I'm sorry. Are you hurt?"

Espie straightened up. "I'm okay," she said in Spanish, too.

He smiled at her and she smiled back. Raul called her. "Esperanza, come help Teresa give me the presents."

Espie hooked her thumbs in the belt loops of her jeans and leaned against the truck. "What's your name?" she asked the boy.

"Pedro Alatore. Yours is Esperanza?"

Espie hated people to call her Esperanza, but she liked the way Pedro said it. Raul called her again.

"You'd better go," Pedro told her.

Espie shrugged. "Come on, there're presents for you in there, too." She was thinking about the pants and shirts she had helped wrap. At the time, she thought they were ugly. But they were better than the mended, faded clothes Pedro wore. Although he had rushed forward with the others, he hesitated now and tried to hide his embarrassment. "Let's go before everything is gone," she told him.

When she reached Raul, he said, "You came down here to help, not get in trouble." The way he said "get in trouble," she knew he meant get pregnant. She smirked. "What's the matter with you?" he asked.

"Man, you're older than I thought," she said, and went inside the small house to help Teresa hand him the presents.

She told Espie, "Make sure you don't give him a man's present if a woman is next in line, or a little boy's if the next person is a girl."

At Raul's direction people had formed a line and, after he checked the code letter on the present, he gave each person the package Teresa or Espie handed him.

There were *gracias* from the adults and squeals from the children as they opened their presents. Raul kept saying *"de nada"*—it's nothing—but Espie knew he loved the attention and, after ten minutes of his phony modesty, she decided to shake him up. She gave him the doll she had wrapped. He glanced at the *b* on the package and gave it to the boy who stood at the front of the line. "This is for you," Raul said in Spanish. The boy smiled and tore away the paper while Teresa gave Raul a present for the woman who was now in front of him.

Espie didn't go back for more packages. She leaned against the door and waited to see what the boy would do. He stared at the black-haired doll and grinned. He looked as though he were going to cuddle it in his arms, but the men's laughter stopped him. He threw the doll on the ground and ran to his mother, who was holding a baby to her breast.

Raul turned to Espie. "You pig!" he said between clenched teeth. He grabbed her hand and pulled her off the truck. "You only came down here to cause trouble."

Espie dug the heel of her sandal into his foot. He yelped and let go of her. "That's what they teach us pigs at the police academy," she said, and moved out of his reach.

Pedro left his place in line. "Are you all right?" he asked in Spanish.

"Yeah, I'm okay." Espie nodded toward the line of people. "Better get back in before Santa Claus sees you." Hurt filled Pedro's eyes. She touched his arm. "Hey, I'm sorry. Go get your presents and I'll wait for you."

He grinned and stepped back into place. Raul was passing out presents again. He glanced at Espie, his face full of hate. The ride home was going to be hell.

Chapter 13

Espie hadn't wanted to embarrass the boy by giving him the doll. And he wasn't embarrassed until the men laughed at him. He was only four or five so he probably hadn't learned yet that taking care of babies "was a woman's job." He'd simply held the doll the way his mother held her babies. Espie looked for him after all the presents had been given out. He was pushing a truck through the dirt with the other boys.

Behind them, women ignored the dust raised by the toys. They cooked in pots or tin cans over outside fires. Most of the houses were built of rotting wood, many with cardboard and tar paper roofs. Chickens pecked at the ground and dogs roamed looking for a handout.

Espie looked around at the houses. Pedro said, "Things are bad here. But people have been telling me about all the jobs in Los Angeles."

Espie thought of the men clustered on corners and the long lines at the welfare office she passed on her way to school. "People have been lying to you," she said.

Music started and a man and a woman began to dance. Every eye was on the dancers. Pedro said, "I have to talk to my mother." He hurried to a sad-faced woman. Two men walked past them and disappeared behind the crowd. Espie didn't see Pedro and his mother. She edged her way to Teresa and asked, "What's the big celebration for?"

"Raul said people always play music for him before he leaves. It's their way of thanking him for helping them."

Espie glanced at Raul. He was watching the dancers, but his eyes occasionally wandered past the crowd, his face tense. A moment later he was smiling and applauding the entertainers. "Time to go," he shouted. The musicians asked him to stay for one more number, but Raul headed for his pickup. "It's a long ride back to Los Angeles. I'll come again. You play your song for me then."

Teresa walked behind him and Espie stayed behind her. Men and women thanked her. A little girl clung to her hand. "Will you come back?" she asked.

"Maybe," Espie said, although she had no intentions of returning. She thought she saw Mrs. Alatore but people hid her quickly from view. Espie climbed in the pickup. She looked for Pedro, but she didn't see him. The truck moved slowly through the crowd and Espie watched people wave until it turned a curve in the road.

"You tramp," Raul said.

Espie clenched her hand into a fist but she couldn't slug him without hitting Teresa, who screamed, "She's not a tramp! Tramps are what you pick up after you finish drinking with your friends."

Raul swerved the wheel to avoid a hole in the road. "Shut up, Teresa."

"You shut up. I'm tired of you telling me what to do. I'm tired of you." She pulled off her wig and threw it in his face. He slammed on the brakes. Espie lurched forward and banged her head against the windshield.

Raul slapped Teresa across the mouth. Cars behind

them honked their horns. Raul moved the truck to the side of the road. "I'll take care of you when we get home," he told Teresa. He leaned over and said to Espie. "I knew you were trouble the first day I saw you. You and that uniform. Stay away from Teresa. She's mine, and she does what I say."

Teresa said, "You don't own me. You'll never own me."

They were at the edge of Tijuana and several people approached the truck. Raul said, "I have to get across the border. You and the mini-pig better not give me trouble." He handed her the wig. "Put it on and smile nice, like you feel real good about doing all that charity."

Teresa took the wig, but she didn't put it on. During a self-defense lesson at an Explorer meeting, the girls had been told, "If you get in trouble, humor the guy. Wait for a chance to get away."

Espie said, "Put it on. It looks great on you."

Teresa rubbed her mouth where Raul had slapped her and looked betrayed, but she put on the wig. Raul moved the truck into the line of traffic. "That's playing smart," he said, and Espie tried to figure out what to do.

The early Saturday night crowd jammed the sidewalks and spilled out into the street. Espie wondered if she could convince the border guards that she and Teresa were in trouble. If Espie asked for help would Raul convince them she was kidding and pass it off as a joke or would he make them believe she was trying to cause trouble? That would be easy to do. Most adults believe teen-agers mean trouble anyway. Would Teresa back her up? She had gotten mad at Raul, but maybe she'd chicken out the way she had when she spilled the milk shake. If Espie tried to convince the inspectors Raul was dangerous and they didn't believe her, she'd have to ride home with him even madder than he was now or stay in Mexico with no money and no way to get home.

The truck had been in stop-and-go traffic, and as they neared the end of town, cars and people thinned out. Not many people were returning to the States this early on Saturday night, but the street kids were still peddling their wallets and things.

Raul said, "We'll be at the border in a few minutes. Smile and look like you had a good time."

Espie said, "Anything you say, Raul." She nudged Teresa so she wouldn't say anything. She stared at Espie, but took the hint.

Raul glanced at her. "What you trying to pull?"

Espie smiled. She remembered her Academy training. "Humor a possible psycopath, play for time." Raul was nuts and Espie didn't want to shake him up. "Nothing. I figure we have to ride back to L.A. together—we might as well be friends." Raul didn't look like he believed her, but he was almost at the customs booth.

Espie read the sign on the booth in front of her. U.S. BORDER INSPECTION STATION. STOP HERE UNTIL CAR AHEAD IS RELEASED.

As the pickup got closer, a smile covered Raul's face. "That's Joe. We got it made." He drove up to the booth and put the car in neutral. "Hey, Joe, how you been? Haven't seen you for a long time."

Joe said, "Fine, Raul." He glanced at Espie and Teresa. "You've got pretty company this trip. Your sisters?"

Anger flitted across Raul's face, but his smile returned instantly. "This is my girlfriend, Teresa Hernandez, and that's her friend Esperanza Sanchez. Esperanza works with the Los Angeles police. Great kid. Always helping somebody." Espie knew if she was going to say something about needing help, she had to say it now. But she couldn't. Joe would never believe she was in trouble. Raul was putting on too good an act.

Joe leaned closer to the window. "You girls born in the United States?" Espie and Teresa nodded. "Do you have anything to declare?" Teresa said no, but Espie didn't know what he meant.

Raul said, "He wants to know if you bought anything in TJ."

"No, I didn't," she said.

Raul said, "And I don't have anything to declare." He shifted, ready to drive away.

"Hold it," Joe said. He wrote something on a piece of paper and put it under the windshield wiper. "Drive it up to the 'pen' for a search, Raul."

Raul kept his smile glued in place. "Hey, what's going on? I've been checked almost every time lately."

Joe said, "Some days we check every car, some days it's every fourth car, sometimes it's every tenth car." He shrugged. "You know how it is. Orders are orders. You just been hitting the booth wrong."

Raul said, "Come on. I told you we weren't carrying anything."

Joe said, "You're holding up the line, Raul. Drive to the 'pen,' please." The voice was polite, but firm.

Raul stepped on the gas and drove into a small building where dozens of car trunks and suitcases were being checked. "The bastard's lying," Raul said.

Espie asked, "What's going on?"

"We're going to get the full search." He turned off the ignition. "Again," he said angrily.

An inspector came up. He took the slip of paper from under the windshield wiper and read it. "Step out, please."

Espie and Teresa got out. Raul did, too. Espie asked. "What are they looking for?"

Raul watched the inspector pull out the front seat. "Drugs, booze, fruit, jewelry, who knows?" He followed the inspector. Raul looked calm, but Espie saw the tension of his body against his shirt.

Cars drove into the "pen" and drove out again, but the inspector continued his search. He went inside the small house on the back of the pickup. "Beautiful," he said.

Raul smiled. "Made it myself," he said, but the words had more anger than pride.

He stayed close to the man. From her place outside the truck, Espie saw the inspector pick up the tops of the seats. He felt around the inside. He checked the rug and tried to pull it up. It didn't move. He ran his hand up and around the windows. Finally, he stepped out of the small house. "You may go," he said.

Raul hopped into the truck. Teresa and Espie got in their side. "Move it," he said.

Teresa said, "They really check you over, don't they?"

"Shut up," Raul said, and drove away before Espie could change her mind about asking for help. But there wasn't any more trouble. He didn't even swear at drivers who cut in front of him. As they got closer to L.A., he even hummed quietly.

When they left the freeway, Espie said, "Teresa's house is on the way to mine. Why don't you drop her off first?" She didn't think he'd go along with it, but she hated to leave Teresa alone with him.

He said, "Yeah, I won't have to double back."

Espie felt Teresa relax beside her. They were only a few blocks from home and Espie still hadn't figured out why Raul had wanted them with him. I'd make a rotten pig, she thought.

Chapter 14

It was a few minutes after seven when Espie got home. Mrs. Garcia and Denise were saying the rosary in Mrs. Garcia's room.

She was on the way to her room when the phone rang. She picked up the receiver. "Hello."

Teresa asked, "You okay?"

"Yeah, I'm okay."

"Thanks for getting me out of that truck first."

"I didn't figure you'd want to be alone with him." Espie sat down on the chair beside the phone. "What are you going to do about him?"

"I'm going to tell him to go to hell."

"When you going to tell him this great news?"

"Tomorrow, I guess. Unless he calls tonight."

"Your folks home?"

"No, they left a note. They're at my aunt's house. As soon as they get back, I'm going to tell them how Raul's been acting. Will you back me up?"

"Sure, but how are you going to . . . ?" Espie stopped.

Teresa asked, "How am I going to what?"

"Nothing. Say, listen, Mrs. Garcia and Denise want to

hear about the trip. I'll talk to you later." She didn't want to ask, "But how are you going to protect yourself from Raul?" She started to hang up, then added, "If you need me, call me, okay?"

"Okay, see you."

"Yeah, see you," Espie said, and hung up.

Denise asked, "Have a good time?"

"The gift-giving part was fun, but I'm not very excited about Mexico."

Mrs. Garcia said, "What you mean you are not excited? This morning you can hardly eat, you are so excited."

"That's before I saw Tijuana."

Mrs. Garcia made a face. "Tijuana is not Mexico. Mexico is Guadalajara, Mexico City, the mountains."

Denise asked, "Everybody like the stuff you brought?"

Espie said, "They're so poor, they'd like anything."

Mrs. Garcia said, "Many poor people live in Mexico, but there are rich ones, too. I work for many before I come here." She sighed as though the idea tired her.

They asked her more questions about the trip and Espie told them the things she had done. But what she really wanted to tell them was the way Raul had acted. She thought about Teresa alone at home. Raul was tired. He wouldn't go back tonight. Or would he? Espie wished she could go stay with Teresa, but all she could do was answer Mrs. Garcia's and Denise's questions and hope Teresa's parents came home early.

Espie had trouble getting to sleep. The day strolled past her closed eyes and kept her mind moving from one thing to another—the crowds in Tijuana where not long ago she had hoped to find her father, Raul's moods, Pedro. Why hadn't he been with the rest of the people when the truck left?

She turned over on her side and pulled the blanket to

her chin. And the poverty. Teresa had told her it was there, but Espie hadn't believed how bad it was until she'd seen it. What hope was there for guys like Pedro?

The next morning she called Teresa before Mass. There was no answer. She tried again after church while Denise went for the menudo, but nobody answered the phone. Espie called every half hour after that. Mrs. Garcia asked, "Who you call all the time?"

"Teresa. I thought I'd go over there, but nobody's home."

"Maybe she go with Raul," Mrs. Garcia said.

"Yeah, maybe," Espie said because she didn't want to explain anything. Mrs. Garcia went outside to work on her flowers. She grew different kinds so she'd always have some in bloom to take to Mr. Garcia's grave. Denise was reading in the living room. Espie went to her room and lay across her bed, but she was up in a minute. Where was Teresa? Espie turned on the television and got some religious program. She switched channels, then turned it off. She dialed Teresa's number again and still got no answer.

She picked up her notebook and began to write. "Attention! Refrigerators are Death Traps!"

Denise looked up from her book, "You doing homework during school vacation?"

"I thought I'd write about unused refrigerators and put the notices on bulletin boards in front of grocery stores. A lot of people read those things."

"Need any help?"

"Yeah, you do the English ones and I'll do the Spanish ones, then I can get them up this afternoon."

Every fifteen minutes she dialed Teresa's number. Where could she be?

122

A few minutes after two the phone rang and Espie grabbed it. Teresa said, "Raul just called."

Espie asked, "Where you been?" Her voice was angry after all the worry.

"That's what Raul asked, but he was madder than you."

"What did you tell him?"

"I told him I had been at my aunt's because my folks had gone to the Valley for some all-day retreat thing."

"You told him you were alone? Did you tell him to find himself an old lady?"

"I told him I wasn't going to be his girl anymore."

"What did he say?"

"The same stuff. I was his and I'd always be his."

"Are the doors locked?"

"Sure they're locked."

Espie said, "Keep them that way and don't let him in."

Teresa said, "You think I'm crazy?"

Espie said, "You were crazy enough to tell him you weren't going to be his girl after you told him you were alone."

Teresa said, "Yeah, that was stupid."

Espie said, "Look, Denise and I wrote notices about kids getting trapped in refrigerators. I'm going to put them up outside the markets, then I'll go to your house. Don't open the door until you're sure it's me."

Teresa said, "When will you get here?"

"I won't be long."

"I'll be watching for you," Teresa said.

Espie went back to the living room and picked up the notices she and Denise had finished. "That was Teresa. I'm going to put these up on the way to her house."

Denise asked, "Anything wrong with her?"

"No, she was at her aunt's house because her folks are

gone for the day." Denise's look told Espie she knew something was going on. Espie had known from the first day she met Denise that she would make a great pig. But Espie had learned to dodge Denise's questions, and she didn't give her a chance to ask any more now. She headed toward the back door. "I'm going to ask Mrs. Garcia if I can eat supper at Teresa's."

Mrs. Garcia said Espie could stay and she hurried to put up the notices. At a couple of the stores she got the whistles and the parrot-like pretty girl, pretty girl from the men who seemed to always be there. She wondered what they'd do if she walked up and kneed a couple of them.

One man looked familiar, but she didn't remember seeing him with the others before. She was halfway up the street when she realized he was the man who had approached Raul at *las posadas*. She remembered how Raul had run from him, and she wondered again why Raul had been afraid of such a small man.

She put up the notices until she ran out of them. She and Denise would have to make more. Espie thought about the Lerners' Christmas without Mark. They probably had bought some of his presents before the accident. What a bummer the day was going to be for them.

She was almost at Teresa's house when she heard an engine start. She looked up just as Raul raced past her in his pickup, his face tight with anger. Espie ran to the house.

The door was slightly open and she pushed it. Teresa was on the floor near the couch. A knife lay beside her and she was covered with blood. Espie felt for a pulse. She ran to the phone, dialed 0, and asked for an ambulance. She almost hung up before she remembered to give her name and address. She raced to the bathroom, grabbed a bunch of towels, and ran back to Teresa. As Espie applied pressure to the wounds, the towels grew crimson. She grabbed a clean one. Where the hell was the ambulance?

Teresa's breathing grew slower and slower. Once Espie thought it stopped. "Teresa," she screamed, and Teresa's chest moved. Espie heard a siren. She applied more pressure. The siren came closer until its scream hurt her ears. It whined down and she heard running footsteps. Two men went down beside her. People gathered at the door and began to crowd into the house. She stood up and walked toward them. "Outside, please. The men need room to work." She moved them away the way her instructor had taught her at the police academy. Espie Sanchez, Explorer, was talking and acting while Espie Sanchez, friend, wanted to scream and go into hysterics.

A police car screeched to a halt. Ron Peters and Gary Horton jumped out. Ron ran up the stairs. "Espie, what happened?"

"Raul stabbed Teresa."

Gary Horton held the crowd back and Peters guided Espie inside. "Who's Raul?"

"Teresa's boyfriend."

"Did you see him do it?"

"No, but I saw him drive away."

One of the ambulance attendants yelled, "Clear it."

Gary Horton's voice grew louder and more urgent. People moved and the attendants picked up the stretcher.

Espie asked, "Where they taking her?"

"County General."

"Can I go with her?"

Ron Peters said, "They'll do all they can for her and I need you here. What's this Raul's last name?" He took a pad from his pocket.

"Torres. He's about thirty-five. Five-ten, a hundred and

sixty pounds. Black eyes. Black hair. Medium length, always neat. No, wait. Today his hair was really messed up."

"Car?"

"A pickup. Light green. I don't know the license number."

Ron Peters nodded. "We'll get that. Anything else you can think of?"

"He lives on Monterey Road." She gave him the number of the duplex.

Officer Peters tore off the sheet and gave it to Gary Horton. "Put out an APB on this guy, will you, Gary? And get a couple of guys from the lab to come check this place out."

Gary Horton went out. People still stood on the porch and the sidewalk, but the crowd had thinned out. Officer Peters said, "Do you know where Teresa's parents are?"

"They're at an all-day retreat somewhere in the Valley."

"I'd better call the rectory and see if anybody knows where they are." The policeman dialed information for the number. Espie took a couple of steps toward the couch. Peters said, "Don't go over there, Espie." She moved back and saw blood where she'd been standing with Ron. She realized it had come from her sandals. She kicked them off before she saw Teresa's blood wasn't only on her shoes, it was all over her clothes and her hands. She shivered and hooked her thumbs in the belt loops of her jeans to keep her hands still.

Ron Peters dialed the rectory number and found out where Mr. and Mrs. Hernandez were. Gary Horton came in with two officers Espie didn't recognize. One of them said, "Came by to see if you needed help."

Peters said, "Things are pretty much under control, but

maybe you can drive Espie home. Espie, this is Machado and Cabrillo."

Espie said hello. She asked Peters, "You going to call Teresa's parents?"

"Right away," he said.

"How can I find out how Teresa is?"

"Call County General's emergency room. Somebody there should be able to tell you."

The man named Cabrillo asked, "Ready to go?"

Espie hesitated. Gary Horton said, "Go on, Espie. There isn't anything you can do here."

She walked past the people and ignored their questions. "What happened? Who did it? Is she dead?" they wanted to know.

She got in the back seat of the police car. Officer Machado picked up his mike, "Eleven Adam twenty-five requesting time and mileage check. Mileage nine-two-five-oh, sixteen, thirty-five hundred hours."

A woman's voice said, "Roger, eleven Adam twenty-five, mileage nine-two-five-oh, sixteen, thirty-five hundred hours."

The car moved away from Teresa's house. Its pink stucco shone in the sun. It could have been any house on any street on a quiet Sunday afternoon, but it was a murder house. It had to be a murder house. Nobody could lose all that blood and live. Espie gave the officers directions, then huddled in the corner of the squad car and cried.

Chapter 15

The police radio crackled incessantly. Espie had learned to decipher the codes while working the desk—juveniles causing a disturbance in front of Lucky's, a man beating up his wife, a liquor store hold-up on Monte Vista. And, of course, the all-points bulletin for Raul Torres, male Latin, about thirty-five, five-ten, a hundred and sixty pounds, black eyes, black hair, driving a light-green pickup.

They were almost at Espie's house when the radio voice said, "Eleven Adam twenty-five, see the man, possible body." The voice gave an address off Monterey Road.

The car picked up speed and stopped in front of Espie's house. Machado was on the mike giving a time and mileage check even before she had closed the car door.

When she walked in the house, Mrs. Garcia looked up from the sink where she was washing pinto beans. She dropped the pan and the beans scattered. "Espie, what has happened?"

Denise stopped halfway through a bite of her apple. "That's blood," she said, and ran to Espie.

"It's Teresa's. Raul stabbed her."

Mrs. Garcia said, *"Madre de Dios."*

Denise asked, "Bad?"

"Real bad." Espie headed for the phone and asked information for the hospital number. She dialed it and got the emergency room.

A man's voice said, "Emergency room, Neil speaking."

"I want to find out about a friend. An ambulance brought her in not long ago."

"What's her name?"

"Teresa Hernandez."

There was a brief silence. "Yeah, here it is. She's in surgery."

"Then she's alive," Espie said, relieved.

"She was when I saw her, but that kid sure was in bad shape."

Espie hung up and dialed the hospital again. This time she asked for surgery. "I'm calling about Teresa Hernandez."

"She's in surgery," a woman told her.

"How long will she be in there?"

"I don't know."

"How is she?"

"Critical," the woman said, and Espie stiffened.

"Will you call me when she comes out?"

"Are you a relative?"

"No, a friend."

"I'm sorry. We only notify relatives. You'll have to check with them."

"But they're not home."

"I'm sorry, that's the rule."

"But . . ." The woman hung up before Espie could say anything else.

She slammed down the phone and said to Denise, "While I change clothes, call Carlos and ask him if he'll take me down there."

Mrs. Garcia said, "We go with you."

Espie pulled off her T-shirt, but she found her jeans stuck to her body at places where she'd gotten most of the blood on her. She'd have to take a shower. She hurried to the bathroom. Her reflection in the medicine cabinet mirror showed her hair and face had blood all over them. She turned on the faucets and got under the water without waiting for it to reach a comfortable temperature. She shivered both from the cold and from the idea of washing blood off. A doctor probably did that every day, but it wasn't a friend's blood. Well, maybe sometimes it was. She poured shampoo in her hair and soaped herself down. She wondered what the doctors were doing to Teresa. She jumped out of the shower and dried herself quickly.

Denise said, "Carlos said he'd be right over."

"I'll be dressed in a minute." She put on a clean shirt and a pair of jeans and was waiting on the porch with Denise and Mrs. Garcia when Carlos drove up.

She told them about the stabbing and how she'd tried to stop the bleeding. She told them about the ambulance attendants and the crowd. She didn't really want to talk about it, but she couldn't help herself.

They got off at the Mission Road turnoff and entered through the large iron gates. They passed by the children's hospital building where, less than two weeks ago, Teresa had said, "I'm going to kill him."

Espie should have done something that night. But what? Mary Parks had told her sometimes even the police couldn't hold a guy. I should have told somebody, Espie thought. But she would've had to fink. Damn it. If there was a code of silence, there should be a code to break it.

Carlos stopped in front of the tall building at the top of the hill. "I'll find a parking place and meet you inside."

Espie started up the stairs. Mrs. Garcia climbed slowly. She told Espie, "You go, we find you."

Espie ran up the steps and pushed open the door. "Where's surgery?" she said even before she reached the reception desk.

"Do you have somebody up there?"

Espie thought she'd get the only relatives bit. "My sister," she said.

The man said, "Down this hall and turn left to the elevator."

Espie turned around and almost bumped into a man behind her. "Sorry," she said, and ran down the hall dodging people. Mrs. Garcia and Denise weren't even in sight yet.

When the elevator door opened, Espie stepped out into a brightly lighted room. Benches lined the walls. Half a dozen people slumped or slept on them. Several looked at her with unseeing eyes. Two men dressed in loose-fitting green shirts and pants pushed a stretcher on wheels past her. A nurse held up a bottle connected to the patient's arm by a tube.

Espie said, "Where's Teresa . . . ?"

Nobody stopped or looked back. A man across the room said, "That's what they do. They only talk to you when somebody dies."

A woman stirred. She'd been sleeping on the bench near the elevator. She opened her eyes, closed them again, and began to snore. Her dress had crept halfway up her thighs. Some glanced at her. Nobody moved to lower her dress. Nobody, in fact, did anything except wait.

The elevator door opened. Mrs. Garcia got out with Carlos and Denise. Denise asked, "How's Teresa?"

A nurse hurried through one set of doors that said NO ADMITTANCE, into another door that said the same thing.

"I haven't been able to talk to anybody."

Mrs. Garcia said, "How we find out?"

Carlos walked to the end of the small hall. The others watched him. He shrugged and came back. "There's nobody down there. I guess we'll have to wait until somebody shows up."

Mrs. Garcia walked to the sleeping woman and pulled down her dress. She had stopped snoring. A nurse came through the doors. "Mrs. Kowalski?" she said before Espie could take a step forward.

A tiny gray-haired woman stood up. She whispered, "He's dead?"

The nurse put her arm around the woman. "His heart was weak, you know." The old woman nodded. "Come with me. I'll find somebody to help you fill out papers and see that you get home."

Espie watched, unable to interrupt. Maybe the man was right. Maybe they only talked to you when somebody died.

But Espie had to know how Teresa was. She stood in front of one of the doors with the NO ADMITTANCE sign and when the door opened, she blocked the nurse's path.

"How's Teresa Hernandez?"

The nurse looked down at Espie. "She's still in surgery. And as long as she's there, she's okay." The woman pushed Espie aside and disappeared behind another door.

Espie regained her balance before she hit the wall. She swore at the nurse. But Teresa was still alive.

They found seats and began the game of waiting with the others. Mrs. Garcia took out her rosary and her fingers worked around it. She was still fingering the beads a half hour later when Teresa's parents stepped off the elevator. Espie rushed to them.

Mrs. Hernandez asked, "How's Teresa?"

"She's still in the operating room."

Mr. Hernandez said, "The police think Raul did this." Espie nodded. Mr. Hernandez shook his head. "He wouldn't hurt her. He loves her."

Espie said, "He loved owning her."

Mrs. Hernandez said, "How can we find out how she is?"

Espie said, "We've tried that. All we've learned is that she's still alive."

Mrs. Hernandez said, "You mean she might die?"

Espie realized Ron Peters hadn't told Mr. and Mrs. Hernandez how badly hurt Teresa was. "Not as long as those doctors work on her."

Espie suddenly felt like she was part of a television show—a bad television show. "Come meet Mrs. Garcia," she said.

While she was introducing everybody, a nurse came out. "Mr. Morgan?" she said. The man who had told Espie the nurses only talked to you when somebody died, jumped up. The nurse said, "Your wife is in the recovery room. You should be able to see her in the women's ward later."

"Thanks," he said, and rang for the elevator. He turned to the others. "Good luck," he said. The sleeping woman stirred and started to snore again.

The nurse was behind the protection of the NO ADMIT-TANCE doors before the Hernandezes had a chance to talk to her.

Espie told them what had happened. Mrs. Hernandez kept saying, "But why?" And while Espie told them how Raul had treated Teresa, Mr. Hernandez interrupted several times with, "I'll kill him."

Mrs. Hernandez said, "I was so afraid she'd get mixed up with a gang."

Espie put her thumbs in the belt loops of her jeans and slumped down on the bench. "Yeah, I know," she said.

Carlos got up. "I'm going to call the station and see if they've caught Raul." He headed toward a phone booth at the end of the hall. As he walked back everybody looked at him. He shook his head. "No sign of him," he said when he reached them.

The nurse Espie had confronted came in. "Miss Hernandez?" she said.

Espie jumped up with Teresa's mother and father. "This is Mr. and Mrs. Hernandez."

Mrs. Hernandez asked, "How is Teresa?"

"Very critical. We're putting her in the intensive care unit. I'm sorry, but that means only the two of you can visit her and you can only see her for ten minutes at a time."

Mr. Hernandez asked, "Why?" Espie remembered Dr. Martinez at the children's hospital and the little boy in the oxygen tent and knew why.

The nurse said, "The fewer people patients in intensive care come in contact with, the less chance they have of getting germs they're too sick to fight."

Mrs. Hernandez asked, "Can we see her now?"

"You'll have to wait until ten. We only let visitors in the ward on the hour. That gives the doctors and nurses fifty minutes to give the patients all the attention they need."

Espie looked at the clock on the wall. It was nine thirty. She had found Teresa around three o'clock. The nurse told Mr. and Mrs. Hernandez, "I suggest you go in at ten to see her, then go home and try to sleep."

Mrs. Hernandez said, "We can't leave her."

The nurse pointed to the woman who had been sleeping on the bench. "She hasn't left the hospital for two days.

She wants us to wake her up every hour so she can see her son, but we've decided to let her sleep tonight so she won't get sick on us." The nurse looked from Mrs. Hernandez to Mr. Hernandez. "Believe me, it's better that you go home. Teresa won't be awake for hours and if her condition changes, we'll call you."

A man's voice came from behind the closed doors. "Nurse." There was no mistaking the urgency. The woman ran and left them all standing there.

Mrs. Garcia said, "We wait with you."

Mrs. Hernandez said, "You don't have to. You all look so tired. We'll see her at ten, then go home like the nurse said."

Espie didn't want to leave, but Mrs. Garcia looked exhausted and Espie realized nobody had eaten since lunch. "Will you call us if there's any change?" she asked, knowing that any change at this point would probably mean worse. And worse than very critical was death.

Mr. Hernandez said, "We'll call you right away."

Mrs. Garcia asked, "You will be okay?"

The Hernandezes nodded and walked with them to the elevator. The woman was still sleeping. Espie wondered when the nurses would wake her up so she could see her son.

They drove home in silence. When they got in the house, Mrs. Garcia said, "I make sandwiches."

Denise said, "You get ready for bed; Espie and I'll make them."

"Thank you. I am very tired."

They had just sat down to eat when the phone rang. "It is about Teresa," Mrs. Garcia said.

The three of them stared at the phone, afraid to answer it.

Chapter 16

The insistent ring of the telephone drew Espie to it. She picked it up. "Hello."

Carlos said, "I just called the station. The Sarge said they found Raul's pickup." Espie was so relieved to hear Carlos's voice, it took her a moment to realize what he had said.

"Where?" she asked.

"On the Santa Ana Freeway, just south of downtown. A car slowed down and he smashed into it."

"Is he hurt?"

"I guess not. He climbed over a guardrail and got away. The Sarge said the front end of the truck is pretty smashed up, but the camper wasn't damaged."

"The camper? You mean the house?"

"What house?" Carlos asked.

Espie realized Carlos had never seen the small house Raul had built. "Instead of using a regular camper shell, he made a house to put on the back of the truck."

"Why did he do that?"

"He likes beautiful things," Espie said. She thought of

Teresa. "He didn't have that on the truck when I saw him drive away from Teresa's house."

"Well, the accident report said it was on there."

"Why would he go for the house if he knew the police would be looking for him?" Espie answered her own question. "He was heading for Mexico and he was going to live in it. He figured he could get over the border before Teresa's parents found her. Where's the truck now?"

"The police impounded it. If I hear anything else I'll call you. And I'll pick you up at two tomorrow. I have roll call at two fifteen."

Espie had forgotten about working the desk the next day. "I don't know if I'll go," she told Carlos.

"You said you would."

"That was before Teresa got stabbed."

"You can't do her any good at home and you can't see her at the hospital," he said.

"Look, I'm really tired. I'll let you know tomorrow."

Espie hung up. Neither Mrs. Garcia nor Denise had taken a bite of their sandwiches. Espie went back to the table and, while they ate, she told them the parts of the conversation they hadn't understood.

Mrs. Garcia said, "The police will catch him."

Denise said, "Where can he hide?"

Espie thought of the description she had given the police. It fit thousands of men in East Los Angeles. "Anywhere in the barrio," she said.

Denise told her, "Too many people know him."

Mrs. Garcia repeated, "The police will catch him." She stood up and moved toward the bedroom. "Now I go pray for Teresa."

Denise headed for her room and Espie followed her. She saw her clothes on the floor where she had dropped them when she'd come back from Teresa's house. They were caked with blood. She hated to touch them, but she couldn't go to sleep with them in her room. She picked them up and brought them to the clothes basket. On her way back to her room she caught a glimpse of Mrs. Garcia on her knees in front of the statues of Our Lady of Guadalupe and Saint Martin de Porres. She went to kneel beside her and they prayed for Teresa together.

The phone woke Espie shortly after six. She ran to it. "Hello."

"Espie?"

"Yes."

"This is Mrs. Hernandez. We just saw Teresa. She was sleeping, but the doctor said she spoke a few words to him during the night."

"How is she? I mean, how does the doctor say she is?"

"I asked him, but he just said she's young and strong and that's probably what's kept her alive. The wound nicked her heart."

"Do you think if I hung around down there long enough, I could sneak in to see her?"

"You wouldn't get by the nurses. They check everybody before they go in. But I'll call you every hour and let you know how she is."

"Thanks," Espie said, and hung up. She went back to her room. Denise was still sleeping. Espie lay down but she couldn't get back to sleep. She wondered if the police had found Raul. She went back to the phone and dialed the police station. "Northeast Division, Officer Benedict speaking, may I help you, please?"

"This is Explorer Sanchez. Has Raul Torres been picked up yet?"

"One moment, please," the man said. He came back on, and said, "There's still an APB out on Raul Torres."

Espie thanked him and hung up. Mrs. Garcia came from her room. "Who you call so early?"

"The station to find out if Raul had been picked up."

"They get him?"

"Not yet," Espie said, and told her about the call from Mrs. Hernandez. "She will live," she said, but she didn't sound as though she believed her own words.

The call from Mrs. Hernandez at seven fifteen didn't give them any encouragement. Denise got up and Espie told her about the calls. They ate breakfast in silence except for one or the other saying Teresa would be all right and the police would get Raul.

Mrs. Hernandez called again at eight fifteen and at nine fifteen. No change. Espie said, "I'll go nuts hanging around here all day waiting for these calls."

Mrs. Garcia said, "I think if you go work on the desk, you feel better." Espie shook her head. "You must be busy."

Espie said she wouldn't go, but when Carlos called at eleven thirty to see if she was going to work the desk, she told him she would. Mrs. Hernandez's hourly calls reported no change and Espie knew Mrs. Garcia was right about being busy. Anything was better than the sitting and waiting.

She found action at the police station. The radio chattered without letup. Officers brought in prisoner after prisoner. People came in with complaints. Espie told Sergeant Jackson, "I thought Christmas was the time of peace and good will toward men."

"It's also the time of shoplifting, drunken driving, fights, and family brawls."

Carlos came to the desk. "I just came from roll call." He tried to sound casual about the briefing, but his voice told her how excited he was. "The Sarge said Raul was seen near Cypress and Division about an hour ago."

"Who saw him?"

"Some citizen coming out of the grocery store."

"Was he sure it was Raul?"

"He made positive identification."

The phone rang. Espie picked it up. Carlos said, "I have to get on the street." He strolled down the hall toward the exit.

Espie spoke into the phone. "Northeast Division, Explorer Sanchez speaking, may I help you, please?"

Denise said, "I've been trying to get through for fifteen minutes. What's going on down there?"

"Everything."

"Mrs. Hernandez called. Teresa talked to her a couple of minutes during the two o'clock visit."

"What did she say?"

"She said she had the doors locked, but Raul got in the back door anyway."

"How?"

"Mrs. Hernandez had given him a key while the men painted the house and she forgot to get it back."

"That was stupid."

"That's what Mrs. Hernandez said."

Sergeant Jackson said, "Espie, take this to homicide, will you?"

Espie told Denise, "I have to go. Call me after Mrs. Hernandez checks in."

Espie picked up the paper Sergeant Jackson had put aside for her and walked across the hall to homicide. Investigator Frank Fallon was talking on the phone. When Espie put the paper on the desk, she spotted a picture in an open folder. "That's Pedro," she said.

Fallon stopped talking into the phone. "You know that kid?" he asked.

"Pedro Alatore. He lives in a village outside TJ. I met him there Saturday."

Investigator Fallon told the person he'd been talking to, "I'll call you back." He hung up and asked Espie, "You sure?"

Espie caught her breath. "He's dead."

"Yeah, we found him and these two men." He shuffled papers and showed her pictures of the two men she had seen Saturday behind the crowd watching the dancers. Frank Fallon said, "The bodies were found yesterday around four in a ravine below Monterey Road." That was the radio call Espie had heard when Machado and Cabrillo were giving her a ride from Teresa's house.

"What happened to them?"

"Carbon monoxide poisoning."

"How did they get up here? They were in TJ Saturday."

The investigator asked, "Who did you go to Tijuana with?"

"Teresa Hernandez and Raul Torres."

Frank Fallon frowned. "Raul Torres," he said slowly, then snapped his fingers. "He's the guy who stabbed some girl yesterday."

"He stabbed Teresa."

Fallon pointed to a chair across from him. "Sit down and tell me everything you remember about Saturday."

Espie sat on the edge of the chair and told him about her trip. When she finished, Investigator Fallon said, "Torres must have brought these guys in."

"He couldn't have. I told you a customs man went through the camper."

"He hid them somewhere." Frank Fallon leaned back in his chair. "I'd sure like to get my hands on that truck and camper."

Espie said, "It's in the impound garage downtown."

Fallon asked, "How did it get there?" When Espie told him, he didn't try to hide his amazement. "Is there anything you don't know about this case?"

"Yes. If Raul brought those guys in, how did he do it?"

Frank Fallon closed the folder and stood up. "Let's go to the impound garage and find out." Espie stared at him. "Come on. I'll fix it up with Sergeant Jackson."

She followed him to the desk. Within minutes she was on her way downtown in the investigator's car, not sure of what she could do to help, but excited that she had a chance to try.

Frank Fallon pulled in the driveway and drove up the ramp to the check-in booth. He filled out a form to show which car he was going to inspect, then cleared Espie with the man on duty. He pointed toward the pickup and they walked toward it, their footsteps echoing through the garage. As they approached the truck, Espie saw the right front fender pushed in against the wheel.

Although she had explained what the camper looked like, Frank Fallon was impressed with the small house. And when he opened the door, he gave a low whistle. Espie said, "I told you, he likes beautiful things."

Frank Fallon didn't bother to look in the cab of the pickup. Instead, he got down and looked under the back of it. He felt the edges, then stood up, stepped back, and looked at the house from all angles. He said, "It doesn't look like it has a false floor."

He got in and started to check the inside the way the customs agent had done, but he gave most of his attention to the floor. "There has to be a sliding floor board," he said while he crawled on his hands and knees on the shag rug. Finally, he stood up and stomped on the floor.

Espie asked, "What are you doing?"

"If there's room for three men, there has to be a hollow area that will sound different than the rest of the camper," Detective Fallon said. But Espie didn't hear a difference and neither did Frank Fallon. He sat down on one of the seats and looked around. "He must have spent months on those wall carvings."

Espie sat across from him. "He did," she said. Suddenly she jumped to her feet. "The roses!"

"That's what I'm talking about," the man said.

Espie started pushing the center of the roses. "No, listen, Raul has this coffee table and when he presses a couple of roses it opens into a game table." Espie pushed a button, then another, and another. One gave to her touch. "Here's one," she said, and started feeling others around her. "The buttons have to be close enough for one person to be able to press both of them at the same time."

Investigator Fallon started pushing the center of the roses, too. "You mean that's how the floor opens?"

"Must be." They pressed rose after rose. Her finger finally pushed in another button. She pressed both at the same time and the center of the rug opened.

Frank Fallon said, "Well, I'll be damned." Espie looked in a hole filled with foam rubber. Fallon said, "That's why there was no hollow sound."

She stared at the space that didn't look big enough to hold three people, but it had. It had been their death trap.

"How did they get poisoned?"

"There must be a hole in the floor or something. I'll get the lab guys down here to check it out and get prints."

He headed for the check-in booth and dialed a number. When he hung up, he said, "They can't come down for a couple of hours. Let's get back to the station. I want to call the customs chief at the border."

As they drove through the heavy traffic and the crowds

of last-minute Christmas shoppers, Espie thought of Pedro's mother. After Fallon called the customs office, somebody would go to the village and explain about Pedro and the two men who died with him. Who were they? They had no identification and Espie didn't know their names. She had noticed them in Mexico only because they weren't watching the dancers like everybody else was. Did they have families? And what had they and Pedro sacrificed to get the two or three hundred dollars each had paid Raul to get across the border?

Espie asked Fallon, "Do you think these are the first people he brought in?"

Frank Fallon shook his head. "I'll bet he brought some in every time he went on one of his charity missions."

"I knew there was something phony about that charity stuff, but I never figured wetbacks. Teresa said he even told her the police should round them all up and ship them back to Mexico."

Frank Fallon stopped for a pedestrian, "It would be the easiest way to get rid of all those people he brought across the border."

"Why would he want to do that?"

"There's always a chance of one of them getting drunk and talking or getting mad because he can't find work."

The car moved again. Espie remembered the man Raul had run away from at *las posadas*. "Yeah, I guess when people think you're the great charitable worker, you don't want all those faces around to remind you you're really a body mover."

They pulled into the driveway beside the station, parked behind the building, and went in the back door. Espie saw Carlos alone in the roll-call room.

"What are you doing off the street?" she asked. Frank Fallon walked toward his office.

144

"Peters and Horton are filling out a report. We got Raul," Carlos said. He stared at the empty coffee cup in his hand.

"Where?" Espie asked with a relief she hadn't felt since she found Teresa.

"In the railroad yard at the bottom of Division." He looked up and Espie saw his face.

"Hey, you don't look so good."

"Raul tried to jump a train and slipped. He's smashed up pretty bad."

"Is he dead?"

"He was alive when they put him in the ambulance."

"They take him to County General?"

Carlos nodded. He stood up and threw his cup in the wastepaper basket. "I'd better get upstairs."

"You going back on the street?"

"I have to. If I'm going to make it as a cop, I can't let things tear me up."

Espie walked with him to the desk, unsure of how she felt about Raul's accident. Ron Peters asked Carlos, "Feeling better?"

Carlos nodded.

Sergeant Jackson said, "Hey, Espie, Denise called. She said Teresa asked about you."

"What did she say?"

"She wanted to know if you were all right."

"Why shouldn't I be?"

"Before he stabbed her, Raul told her he was going to kill you."

Everybody stared at Espie. The phone rang. She picked it up. "Northeast Division, Explorer Sanchez speaking. May I help you, please?" she said, and was surprised that her voice could be so steady when her whole body was shaking.

Chapter 17

The woman on the other end of the line answered Espie's polite offer for help with, "No, you can't help me. Give me a policeman." Espie didn't even try to reason with her. She remembered the woman's voice. She turned to Sergeant Jackson.

"Mrs. Caldwell," she said.

Sergeant Jackson sighed and picked up his phone. "Yes, Mrs. Caldwell."

Espie asked Ron Peters. "Think Raul will live?"

"If he does, he won't be able to hurt you. They'll have him locked up a long time."

Espie picked up a stack of folders. "I have to take these to Officer Parks."

As she went out the door, she heard Sergeant Jackson say, "Okay, Mrs. Caldwell, I'll tell the boys to stop by for Christmas cookies."

Parks looked up when Espie came in. "Hi. All ready for Christmas?"

Espie shrugged. "What's there to get ready?"

"Presents. Did you get Mrs. Garcia something?"

"I'm going to give her a terrarium. The bottle is shaped

like a violin and when the sun shines on it, the glass looks pink."

"Sounds beautiful. Where'd you get it?"

"Raul made it." Espie dropped the folders on the officer's desk. "I can't give that to Mrs. Garcia after what he did to Teresa."

"What did he do?"

"He stabbed her."

"When?"

"Yesterday. She's in the intensive care unit at County General."

"Did we pick him up?"

"Peters and Horton got him a couple of hours ago. He's at County General, too. He slipped trying to hop a train."

"How badly is he hurt?"

"Pretty bad."

"I don't understand. Why can't you give Mrs. Garcia the terrarium?"

"He made it." Espie said, and sat down.

Mary Parks leaned back in her chair. "We're closing the Christmas tree lot at six and a couple of the off-duty officers and I are going to take baskets of food and the leftover trees to some of the families in the precinct. Why don't you come with me and I'll drop you off at home when we finish?"

"Okay. Carlos is with Peters and Horton on the ride-along program. I won't get home until after eleven if I wait for him, and Mrs. Garcia wants to go to Midnight Mass." Espie headed for the door and stopped. "Will you call the hospital and find out about Raul? I don't want to ask Sergeant Jackson."

Officer Parks checked her phone book and dialed. When she finished her call, she told Espie, "He's in the prison ward in satisfactory condition."

"I guess he's not going to die."

"For some people, there are worse things than dying," Parks said.

"Yeah," Espie said, and went back to the desk wondering if Raul was conscious enough to remember what he'd done to Teresa.

Carlos, Ron Peters, and Gary Horton had left. She said to Sergeant Jackson, "Did you take care of Mrs. Caldwell?"

"Yeah, she wants the guys to come by for some cookies. I told you she was just a lonely woman." He kept his eyes on Espie's face. "You've had a rough twenty-four hours, haven't you?"

"Rough enough," she said, and was glad to see a man come in so she wouldn't have to continue the conversation.

The man said, "I've been robbed," and Espie wrote down the information he gave her. The phone rang several times while he was there and it continued to ring after he left. It kept her so busy, she didn't think about Denise's report about Teresa. When it came Denise said, "The doctor told Mrs. Hernandez Teresa is making such progress, he may move her to a regular ward later tonight."

"Hey, that's great! Maybe I can see her."

"Maybe," Denise said, and Espie was so excited she forgot to tell Denise about Raul. She started to dial her home number when Frank Fallon interrupted her.

"I finally got a report from the Border," he told her. Espie put down the phone. "The inspectors had been keeping a close watch on Raul because four months ago he was asked to drive to the 'pen' for a routine check and the inspector thought Raul acted kind of nervous. The guy couldn't find anything so he passed the word along to check out the pickup and camper more often."

148

Espie asked, "Why do you think Raul wanted Teresa and me to go with him Saturday?"

"I asked the customs guy about that and he said he thought Raul figured they wouldn't hassle him if he had a couple of kids with him." Espie's face tensed. Fallon smiled. "Sorry. I mean a couple of young women. The guy was really interested in how those roses worked."

"Did they suspect wetbacks?"

"He said they figured if Raul was carrying anything, it was narcotics."

"I guess somebody's gone to the village to tell Pedro's mother."

"Yeah, and find the families of the other two victims. It's going to be a hell of a Christmas."

Espie nodded. Sergeant Jackson had been right. She had been through a rough twenty-four hours. But the worst was over for her. The holiday would be a real bummer for Mark's and Pedro's families and the families of those two men.

"Did you get a report from the lab men on the camper?"

"No, but after the story you told me, I figure we'll have enough physical evidence to charge Raul with manslaughter, at least."

The phone rang and Frank Fallon waved. "Merry Christmas," he said, and Espie waved back.

It was a routine complaint about kids driving cycles on the hills by Occidental College, and Espie took down the information.

A few minutes after six, Mary Parks came to the desk with baskets of food. "Take these out to my car, will you, Espie, and I'll get some more from my office."

Sergeant Jackson said to Espie, "Hey, you deserting me?"

Parks said, "Sorry about that, Ernie, but there're people out there who won't have anything to eat tomorrow if we don't get these baskets to them."

They made dozens of trips before they had all the baskets in the Christmas tree lot where a couple of cops had loaded trees in their vans and in Parks's station wagon. Espie went back to the desk for her hat. "Have a nice Christmas," she told Sergeant Jackson.

"Yeah, you too," he said as he reached for the ever-ringing telephone.

Mary Parks made sure the guys had their lists of names and addresses, then climbed in her car. Espie was glad to get in out of the wind. Parks started the car. "I'll get the heater on in a few minutes."

"Thanks," Espie said, and she hugged herself to keep warm. There were presents on the seat and on the floor beside her feet. "Who are these for?"

"The kids. I couldn't see giving them a tree without presents to put under it so I took up a collection from everybody I could corner and bought some things."

"Hey, that's great," Espie said, feeling like it just might be a nice Christmas.

The first house they stopped at was over a store near Avenue 33. Parks said, "This man's been in the hospital for months. He's home now, but he can't work. One of the neighbors told us about the family." Parks handed Espie four small presents. "Here, you take these and the food and I'll get the tree."

Espie stepped out in the cold and shivered. She climbed up steps along the outside of the building and waited while Parks came up with the tree. It wasn't very big, but she'd put a foil star on the top and it glistened in the glow from the street light.

Parks knocked and a small boy opened the door. He

stood silent and motionless, then let out a jabber of Spanish that brought three other children and a thin, short woman. "Go. I have no money," she said.

Parks told her, "We don't want money, Mrs. Navarro. We want to give you these."

The children were all talking at once. A man's voice came from the other room. "What's going on?" he asked in Spanish.

The woman's eyes settled on the chicken and the other food in the basket. "Why?" she asked.

"Because it's Christmas," Mary Parks said, and stepped past the woman to put down the tree. Espie set the food and the presents under it and went back to the door."

"Merry Christmas," Espie said. Mary Parks repeated the greeting and they closed the door without another word.

"Wow," Espie said on the way down the stairs because she couldn't think of anything else to say about the few moments of happiness and the days of misery the Navarros faced.

Espie and Mary Parks grew more silent after every stop. There was just so much they could say about the poverty they saw and people's reactions to the surprise visits. After they delivered the last packages, Mary Parks asked why Raul had stabbed Teresa. Espie told her about the trip to Mexico and about finding Teresa. Parks said, "First Mark, then Teresa. You're getting your nurse's training before you even take a class."

"I'm not going to be a nurse."

Parks glanced at her. "Why not?"

"I get too scared. I mean . . ." She hated anybody to know she got scared.

"Everybody gets scared sometimes."

"Do you?"

"When I was working juvenile, I was scared almost every day."

"Then why did you keep doing it?"

"Because I was good at it." Mary Parks turned onto Daly Street. "And you'd be a good nurse."

"How do you know?"

"Because of the way you reacted to Mark and Teresa. You may have been scared, but you did what you'd been taught to do. That's the sign of a pro."

They stopped in front of Espie's house. She sat with her hand on the door handle. "It is?" Parks nodded and Espie opened the door. "Good night," she said.

Parks said, "Merry Christmas."

Espie said, "Yeah, thanks," and hurried in out of the cold.

It was eight thirty and Espie asked Denise what Mrs. Hernandez had said when she called at eight fifteen.

Denise said, "She didn't call."

"Did she call at seven fifteen?"

Denise nodded. "She told me Teresa had slept during the ten-minute visit."

Mrs. Garcia said, "She is all right."

Denise said, "Sure she is. The doctor said he might put her in a regular ward, didn't he?"

Espie said, "I guess you're right," but it worried her that Mrs. Hernandez hadn't called.

Mrs. Garcia asked, "Did the police find Raul?"

Espie realized she'd been so busy at the station, she hadn't completed the call Frank Fallon had interrupted. She told Mrs. Garcia and Denise what had happened to Raul, then told them about Pedro and the two men. Neither Mrs. Garcia nor Denise said anything except for Mrs. Garcia's occasional *Madre de Dios*.

When Espie stopped talking, Denise said, "I've been a L.E.E.G. over a year and the most exciting thing that happened to me was a fight that broke out at the Franklin Heights carnival."

Espie told her, "Yeah, well, I've had all the excitement I need for a long while."

Mrs. Garcia said, "But Espie, you must have more excitement. It is Christmas Eve. There are presents to open."

Espie glanced at the stable surrounded by things Mrs. Garcia had received from her foster children. A cardboard carton with "Soup 24 cans. This side up" printed on it was beside them. The package Raul had wrapped for Mrs. Garcia was in front of it.

Espie said. "Who put that there?"

Denise said, "I did. I figured since Christmas was tomorrow, I'd get it out."

"But I wasn't going to . . ." The phone rang and Espie picked it up. "Hello."

Mrs. Hernandez said, "Espie?"

"Why didn't you call at eight fifteen? Is something wrong?"

Mrs. Hernandez laughed. "Somebody wants to talk to you."

Teresa said, "Hi, Espie."

Espie was too stunned to speak. Finally, she said, "Hey, how are you feeling?"

"Weak. I can't get out of bed. But I hassled the doctor until he let me make this call on my way from intensive care to the regular ward. I wanted to thank you."

"Forget it," Espie said, then realized that sounded stupid when it was a life she was talking about. "I mean, I just happened to be there."

Espie heard whispering in the background. Teresa said, "I have to go. Can you come see me tomorrow? My father will pick you up."

"Sure, I'll come."

"Okay, see you."

"See you," Espie said. She hung up and shouted, "Merry Christmas."

Mrs. Garcia said, "Teresa is all right?"

"Sounds like she's going to be," Espie told her.

Denise imitated Espie's Merry Christmas and they all laughed.

Mrs. Garcia said, "Every year we open the presents Christmas morning, but this time we open them Christmas Eve."

Denise asked, "How come?"

Mrs. Garcia smiled. "You will see."

Denise gave Mrs. Garcia the package with the votive candle. After she opened it, she said, "Just what I need. My other one is almost finished."

Denise said, "I know," and gave Espie a small gift-wrapped box.

Espie asked, "What's this?"

"Open it and see."

Espie said, "I didn't get anything for you."

Mrs. Garcia said, "That does not matter. Christmas is for love, not for presents."

Espie tore off the paper and took a key chain out of the box. Denise said, "I made it in school."

Espie turned the small leather key holder over and saw the letter *E* on it. "Gee, thanks. It's great." Ideas raced through her mind. Suddenly she ran to the phone and wrote on the pad beside it, "The next five times we have to do the dishes I'll wash and you can wipe. Merry Christmas." She went back to the couch and gave it to Denise.

Denise read it and laughed. "It's a deal." She showed it to Mrs. Garcia.

"That is a nice present," she said.

Denise said, "Give Mrs. Garcia her present."

Espie hesitated, then picked up the package. Mrs. Garcia said, "That beautiful present is for me?" Espie nodded and Mrs. Garcia carefully took off the bow and paper. "I save for next year," she said. When she saw the terrarium, she held it level to her eyes and turned it around and around. "Espie, where you get such a present?"

"Raul fixed it," Espie said, keeping her eyes on Mrs. Garcia's face.

"It is beautiful. Thank you." She pointed to the cardboard box. "That one is for you. I am sorry I did not have paper to wrap it," she told Espie.

Espie said, "That big one is for me?" Mrs. Garcia smiled. Espie grabbed it and pulled at the string. It finally broke and she opened the cardboard flaps. She pulled out the cloth folded inside. "A coat," she shouted. She held it away from her. It was navy blue with brass buttons. She hugged Mrs. Garcia. "Thank you," she said, and put on the coat while she ran to the bedroom to look in the mirror. It fit perfectly.

When Espie went back to the living room, Denise was taking a green dress out of a box. "It's my favorite color," she said.

Mrs. Garcia told her, "That is why I make it." She stood up. "We go to Midnight Mass now?"

Espie put her hands in her pockets and clutched the coat to her. "At last I'll be warm," she said.

"I wanted to give it to you before but I . . ." She shrugged and Espie knew there had been no money for the coat or for Denise's dress until Mrs. Garcia had done twice as much sewing as she usually did.

When they got outside, the wind whipped around the corner and brushed a palm frond across Espie's cheek. Mrs. Garcia asked her, "You are warm enough?"

Espie nodded. She huddled in her coat and prayed she'd never be cold again.